BEWITCHED

BREAKERS HOCKEY #5

ELISE FABER

BEWITCHED
BY ELISE FABER
Newsletter sign-up
This is a work of fiction. Names, places, characters, and events are fictitious in
every regard. Any similarities to actual events and persons, living or dead, are
purely coincidental. Any trademarks, service marks, product names, or named
features are assumed to be the property of their respective owners, and are used
only for reference. There is no implied endorsement if any of these terms are
used. Except for review purposes, the reproduction of this book in whole or
part, electronically or mechanically, constitutes a copyright violation.

ONE

Raph

I PUSHED MY DRINK AWAY, knowing that if I finished it, I would get sloppy.

I didn't *get* sloppy.

Nope.

I abided by a careful recipe of drinking at CeCe's, consuming enough food, and stopping at just the right time to prevent me from getting *sloppy*.

A pinch of this. A dash of that. Two stirs. And *ta-da!*

The patented Raphael Gomez recipe to pretend my life wasn't a shit-show.

Drown out the voices in my head.

But do it in a way that didn't bring any intervention from my teammates—who would definitely have my back *and* take it upon themselves to clear up my shit, or worse, Hazel might take notice. Or take *more* notice. Already, sometimes the team psychologist looked at me as though she could see through the shield I'd erected.

And I couldn't have that.

I was too busy shoring up that shield, barricading myself behind it, too busy letting the hurt and betrayal eat through every inch of me, to gnaw at my very bones.

Sighing, I threw some bills on the bar top, started to push away from the bar, ready to go home to my empty house, with the empty rooms, the doors perpetually closed.

"Raph!"

A shiver down my spine.

Fucking hell.

Not *her*.

Anyone but *her*.

Except, even as I turned, I knew it was going to be her. Going to be...Beth.

Fucking.

Hell.

My hands shook, fingers clenching into fists, lungs seizing.

I'd been avoiding her like the goddamned plague. Mostly because she was beautiful and loud and pushy, and I didn't want her in my business, didn't want *any* woman in my business. I'd been there, done that, got the fucking souvenir broken heart from Hurricane Monica.

Or maybe Hurricane Lying Bitch was more accurate.

Monica had lied about something so fucking big that I didn't know how I was ever going to trust another woman.

Ever.

Especially one as beautiful as Beth.

Monica had been gorgeous, impeccably dressed, her makeup always done—high maintenance at its best, and maybe that made me a dick who'd deserved what was coming to me, but I'd always liked my women a little high-maintenance.

Beth was just as gorgeous, just as put together, *and* she was a total ballbuster (something else that used to make me hard).

But I hadn't been avoiding her because of the way she looked or her personality or how she wore her makeup or did her hair or dressed.

Or at least, not *only* those reasons.

The biggest one...the one that my eyes dropped to, so obvious it was impossible to keep my gaze on her face, was leading her charge my way.

The soft rounded curve of her belly.

The babies inside.

Fuck.

That sliced fucking *deep*.

Because I hadn't seen that with Monica. Because she'd lied about carrying my baby. Because...she'd never been pregnant at all. I hadn't seen her belly grow, hadn't felt our baby move, hadn't held my son or daughter in my arms.

How in the fuck was I grieving for a baby that had never even existed?

It didn't make any sense.

But I was.

And it was slicing me deep inside, fucking killing me that Pru and Marcel were going to have two. *Two* babies that Beth was carrying for Pru because she couldn't and—

I was a fucking asshole.

Everyone on the Breakers knew the story, knew that Pru had been attacked traumatically as a child, that she'd lost her parents and parts of her body. We all knew she had barely survived and that it was lucky she was here so we could know her.

And I...*I* knew that Beth was doing something wonderful by carrying Pru and Marcel's babies.

But every time I looked at her, I felt sick to my stomach.

Unfortunately, that evening, there was nowhere to escape— not without looking like a douche, anyway. I might have douchebag thoughts and be a total asshole behind the shield, but I tried not to let that bleed out onto the people around me.

So...I waited for her to come near, and when she smiled and started to hop onto the stool next to me, I helped her up, ignoring the zing the contact brought to my fingertips.

It had been more than a year since I'd touched—yeah *touched*—a woman.

A fucking *year*.

I hadn't been able to bring myself to touch one—not as a friend, not as a woman I wanted to have beneath me in bed. Not since Monica had fucking destroyed me with some internet-bought ultrasounds and a determination to go the long run with her lies.

But...I'd touched Beth. No. *Was* touching her, holding her steady as I waited until I was certain her body had made it safely up onto that stool and wasn't going to tumble down.

She was carrying precious cargo, and I might be a dick on the inside because that fact killed me, but I at least tried to look out for the people in my life, especially those with short legs and who might have an impaired sense of balance because they were carrying twins.

But the feel of Beth's silky skin beneath my fingertips, how she smelled—floral and fruity—how she cradled her little bump, as though protecting the babies inside her womb from the outside world...reminded me.

Some of Monica and how she'd been.

Some of how she hadn't.

Plenty of fruit and flowers and silk. No protective cradling.

No baby.

I clenched my free hand into a fist again, waited for Beth to settle so I could pull back.

But before I could, she turned to face me. "Thank God,

you're here," she exclaimed. "It's not Cheese Night Extravaganza, but I'm starving and losing my mind because I *need* mozzarella sticks." She smiled, glanced down. "Okay, these babies are growing, so *they* need them, but since they're going in my mouth, *I* need them and—"

She broke off, cheeks flushing prettily.

Probably able to see how much her mentioning babies hurt me.

Because Beth was smart—pretty and funny and loud and high maintenance and *fucking* smart.

That made her dangerous, and her next words proved it.

"Sorry," she whispered, her hand lifting, resting on mine. "I didn't think. That was really..." She nibbled on her red-painted lip, but her eyes held mine. "Inconsiderate," she finished, pulling back, forcing me to drop my hand. Which was a good thing.

The smart and *safe* thing.

Her gaze hit on the money on the bar, and her teeth nibbled that red-painted lip again, eyes filling with something I didn't want to examine too closely. "I should let you go. I'll wait for a table—"

"What do you want to eat?" I asked gruffly. "Besides the mozzarella sticks," I added when she lifted her brows, probably to tell me that she wanted fried cheese and she wanted it right then. "Something with at least a *bit* of nutritional value."

"Umm..." Her nose wrinkled. "Nachos?"

A curl of amusement in my chest.

And hell, it had been so long since I'd felt that emotion that it took me a minute to recognize what it was.

I rubbed the ache there, smothered a smile.

God. When was the last time I'd smiled?

"They have vegetables on them," she added a bit mulishly.

Probably because I hadn't responded, given that it had taken me a long fucking time to recognize the emotion of *amusement,* that I was still recovering from the onslaught of feeling like myself for a moment.

"Salsa's not a vegetable," I said once I'd gotten it together.

Her blue eyes narrowed, her long red hair twitched when she spun slightly to face me. "Peppers are. *Olives* are. And guacamole is just a mushed up one."

"Olives are technically fruit."

Those eyes narrowed further.

"Same goes for peppers."

A deeper glare.

"And avocados, too."

She tossed up her hands.

And that amusement in me grew.

But I didn't do anything about it, just bit back my grin and waved down the bartender, put in an order for a club soda, nachos, mozzarella sticks, *and* a side of fruit.

When the bartender went to plug that into the register, I turned back to Beth.

Who was staring at me with wide eyes. "You know what I drink?"

I knew a lot about her—too much considering I'd spent the better part of a year building my shield against her. I knew what she drank. I knew that she was a good friend, that her ass was incredible and frequently featured in tight skirts. I knew that she ate too much junk food and that if I'd ordered a salad, she wouldn't touch it, but that she *would* deign to eat the fruit in the name of something healthy.

But I couldn't reveal any of that, could I?

So, I just said, "I've hung out with you, Hazel, Pru, and company enough. I know what you *all* drink."

That dropped her brows, though a thoughtful expression took the place of her surprise. "Right," she whispered.

We sat in silence—or rather, *I* sat in silence—as we waited for her food to come. She prattled on about some TV show the girls were trying to get the guys to watch (but had so far been unsuccessful) and when I didn't bite, she moved on to discussing the team. That was a more interesting conversation—hockey was easy. Hockey made sense. But I couldn't bring myself to do more than sit silently next to her.

That was all I had in me.

Thankfully, her food eventually came and because I was sitting next to her and couldn't resist the crispy golden brown deliciousness, I stole a mozzarella stick with the lightning-fast reflexes of a professional hockey player, earning a glare in return for my antics, though she didn't comment.

And eventually, she wore me down.

I found myself joining in her conversation, not just listening to her talk at me, biting back my chuckles at her funny quips and stories and antics, but *actually* talking.

Somehow, *actually* enjoying myself.

And paying for her meal before she could, even though that sent her back to glaring.

For a few moments anyway.

Because then she murmured a "thank you" that I felt deep behind my shield and went back to regaling me with her stories and quick one-liners.

Then the plates were empty, and she was yawning, telling me she should head home.

I stood, put out an arm to help her down from her stool.

Touching. Again.

My fingers tingling. My nerves prickling. My dick—

"And I—"

She broke off, her face going pale the moment her feet hit the floor.

"Beth?" I asked, reaching out with my other arm, wrapping it around her when she wavered.

"What's—"

She took a step.

Her eyes rolled back.

And...she collapsed.

TWO

Beth

"BETH!"

It was bright and loud, and I was dizzy.

Hell, I'd been so dizzy all the time lately.

Gentle hands were coasting over my body—up my arms, over my throat, cupping my face and shaking my head lightly.

"Beth, sugarpie," came Raph's voice. "Wake up."

"Honeybunch," I managed, groaning and reaching a hand up, rubbing my head.

"What?" he asked.

The song was playing through my head, which wasn't really a surprise. I heard music in my mind all the time—oldies like the Four Tops ballad that Raph calling me sugarpie had triggered, new pop songs by badass women, 80's rock by dudes who had better hair than I had. Pretty much anything with a good beat and lyrics that had me bobbing my head and something that pulled me out of myself and into a life that wasn't my own.

Another shake. "*Beth.* Honey, open your eyes."

The song faded, taking second fiddle to the musical quality of Raph's voice. A velvet rasp that should belong to a rock star, vibrating over my skin, making love to my eardrums, sliding up and between my legs—

I was on the floor of a bar.

My lids flew open, light and noise assailing me, all of it coming at once, making me realize that I was sprawled across Raph's lap.

In the middle of CeCe's.

Oh, fuck.

How freaking embarrassing.

Immediately, I tried to push off him, tried to get to my feet. Fresh air. Wait till I was one hundred percent. Drive home.

Good plan.

Only one problem.

Raph's hands closed on my shoulders, pressed me back down into that big, broad lap, and he ordered, "Don't move."

Already, my head was clearing, as seemed to typically happen with these spells, and I wanted to be up on my feet, out of CeCe's, and, seeing as how the entire staff seemed to be gathered around me and Raph, peeking around his billboard-wide shoulders, I was planning on avoiding it for the next half-century.

"I'm fine," I said softly, shifting again, wanting off Raph's lap.

I knew he didn't like me.

I knew it wasn't all just me. Being in Hazel and Pru's circle meant that I'd learned plenty about the guys over the years, not the least of which was the sad story about Raph and his ex, and it was mainly sad because his ex had been a total bitch who'd faked a pregnancy. Who did that?

See? Bitch. Totally, *completely* so.

Especially, when I, in my limited experience there in Baltimore (it was before I'd moved to town from NYC) could see that Raph had been excited about being a daddy.

Why someone would lie about that I would never understand.

But Raph hadn't liked me before his relationship went wrong, before I'd become a surrogate and added salt on a painful wound.

Nope.

I'd felt his dislike from our first meeting.

And I'd done my damndest to get him to change his mind.

I'd been on the boards of charities for a long time, my main gig raising money. I *knew* how to get people to like me, to like me enough to give me money (and that was a feat in and of itself). But I didn't know how to get Raph to like me.

I also didn't know why I kept trying.

Justin Bieber's *Love Yourself* began playing through my head, something I really didn't need right then.

Not with Raph staring down at me, face hard, lips pressed flat. "I said, *don't move.*"

Love myself.

Sure.

Right.

More like *Trouble* by Ray LaMontagne.

My lips parted. Yeah, definitely trouble. Definitely a rasping, rough voice skating over my skin, tingling through my nerve endings, making me do stupid shit like repeatedly throwing myself into his path, hoping that he might like me.

Wasn't going to happen back then.

Wasn't going to happen now, not with two babies in my belly, stretch marks already erupting on my belly, and the worst gas in the history of gas.

And that didn't even include the night sweats, the belly

button that had turned into one of those button things that popped up when a turkey was done cooking, and a difficulty staying awake past nine at night.

I was a total catch.

Yup. *Totally*.

"Beth?"

I blinked, focused back on his eyes. There was a note of something there, and it wasn't his usual annoyance, but before I could really suss out what it meant, it was gone, his gaze going hard again.

"Don't. Move."

My breath slid out, disappointment battling with annoyance.

But since it felt nice—just a little bit—to be in his arms, I stayed in place as he shifted to the side, his arm clamping around my middle.

That was nice, so nice that I didn't immediately process what all that shifting had wrought.

I did, however, hear him say, "Marcel. Raph. I need you to meet me at the hospital. I'm with Beth and she collapsed at CeCe's and—"

"What?" I shook my head, trying to sit up, and when his arm just tightened again, keeping me in place, I began waving my arms. "I'm fine. We don't need to go to the hos—"

"She's conscious now. Was maybe out for thirty seconds. No," he added, seemingly to a question that Marcel had asked. "Didn't hit her head or stomach. I caught her before she could and—" He paused, listening, and then his eyes sliced to mine.

"Any bleeding or cramping?" he asked.

Fuck. Now *that* was embarrassing.

"Let me talk to him," I said, putting my hand out for the cell.

His eyes sliced to mine, the pale blue depths having gone

full Ice Man. "Any bleeding or cramping?" he repeated, enunciating each word in a way that had icy fingers sliding down my spine.

"No," I bit out.

"No." A pause. "Right. We'll be there in fifteen."

He clicked off, shoved his cell in his pocket, but didn't drop his arm. Nope, he kept that big old tree trunk wrapped around me, right beneath my breasts, reminding me that we were currently—and had been from the moment the babies had implanted themselves into my uterus—needy bitches.

"I'm—"

"Not another fucking word," he snapped, standing with me in his arms. "Pru and Marcel went through too much to have these babies for you to jeopardize—"

"I—"

"Not. One. More. Word."

Temper.

Mine.

It was hitting the red zone, and considering that I'd spent my career in fundraising and had dealt with a lot of fucking annoying people and the shit they could shovel on me, that was saying something. Considering that I'd been trying to get this man to like me, to pay attention to me, to touch me for the better part of three years, that was saying *more* than something.

That was saying *everything*.

I didn't often hit the red zone or lose my temper.

Everything rolled off my back. I was adaptable as shit. I could take a flurry of hits and keep on smiling and joking.

This interaction had me turning into a cartoon thermometer, the top trembling and expanding as the mercury within heated up and threatened to burst free.

Deep breaths.

"Please put me down," I said firmly. Quietly, calmly, but *firmly.*

He'd just reached the hall—turn left and we would hit the bathroom, turn right and we'd walk through another large room filled with high-top tables and another wooden bar that took up one wall of the space, the front door at its opposite end. He stopped. "I *said*—"

"I know what you said," I interrupted icily, "and I don't like your tone, nor do I like how you're acting."

His expression was a lesson in anger. "Pru and Mar—"

My eyes suddenly stung, hurt blazing through me.

Because to insinuate—no, to say *outright* that I'd do something to jeopardize these babies—well, he might as well have taken a two-by-four to my stomach...then wound up and struck again. I was giving up my body, my time, my life, and my job in New York—

No, the last two I'd given up willingly, ready for an escape.

Hell, *all* of it I'd given up willingly.

Because Pru was Pru and she'd been handed too much shit in her life and I was happy to do this for my friend. Because I was happy to start my life over somewhere fresh, with a new job and a new house and a place that wasn't full of memories that sliced and clung deep and—

I pushed that aside, lifted my chin. "I would never do anything to hurt these babies."

His brows rose, but he didn't respond, just kept walking down the hall, not giving a fuck that we were drawing plenty of curious stares and not giving a damn that I was dying a slow embarrassing death.

First, tumbling to the floor.

Second, a fucking princess being carried through the bar.

Cute.

"Wait!"

Raph stopped, turned us back slightly and I saw Julie, our favorite server, rushing toward us. She had a to-go cup in one hand and my purse and jacket in the other.

"I wouldn't," I whispered. Begged, really.

If he was insisting on carrying me, at the very least he could keep moving, could end my crippling embarrassment, could put me out of my misery.

But nope.

He stayed still, slanting a glance down at me, his eyes still frosty as Julie caught up to us. Jules handed me the cup and gently tucked my purse in the valley created from my body touching Raph's before spreading my coat over the top. "Water," Jules murmured. A squeeze of my hand. "Feel better, okay? I need you here for Cheese Night Extravaganza next week."

I forced a smile. "I never miss an opportunity for cheese."

"Thanks, Jules," Raph said gruffly, abruptly turning for the front door and pushing through it. He glanced down at me. "No fucking lip. You're going to get checked out."

I sighed. "I know what I'm doing—"

"*I* know that if a pregnant woman passes out, she should go to a fucking doctor, whether or not the babies are her own!" he yelled into the cool night air.

That thermometer burst and my temper let loose "Fuck, man," I snapped. "Fucking *listen* to me and stop interrupting! I'm not dumb or stupid or some fucking little princess you get to boss around." I shoved hard at his chest, managing to loosen his grip enough to wriggle my legs down and get my feet on the ground. "All I've been *trying* to say—if you'd fucking let me talk, that is—is that my doctors are aware of the dizziness. I've mentioned it, and they're not overly concerned, but," I added quickly and loudly when he opened his mouth to no doubt retort back at me, "I'll phone the on-call doc, see what they want me to do. If that's to go into the ER, fine. I'll go. But if they advise something else, then I'm going to listen to the fucking doctor and not some bully of a hockey player who thinks he can treat me like shit just because some pathetic bitch of a female fucked him over!"

I was yelling now.

On a street corner.

Into that cool night air.

Gaining an audience here, too.

Great.

Just pile that right onto my embarrassment, make it even more difficult to carry.

A flash of anger. "I know—"

"You don't know *shit*," I hissed, shoving at his chest before stepping back, gathering my purse and jacket from the ground where they'd fallen due to my squirming, trying to hold them and the cup and not douse myself with the cold liquid. "You don't know *me*. You clearly don't know who I am inside or what I'd do for Pru and Marcel. And you don't—"

I'd taken a step, intending to head to my car, to sit in the driver's seat and make that call.

But then I got dizzy again.

And I wavered.

Turning back, I plowed back into Raph's hard chest, wrapping my arms around him.

Confusion in his bright blue eyes.

"You don't get to be a jerk to me," I whispered, leaning against him.

Silence.

A tense body against mine for just one second. Then his arms wrapped around me.

"You do, however," I said, still whispering, "get to hold me until my head stops spinning and *then* I'll call the doctor."

THREE

Raph

FUCKING SAVE me from fucking stubborn ass women.

She was in the passenger's seat of my car as I drove her to the hospital she'd bitched about me taking her to just ten minutes before.

This being after she'd bickered with me about sitting in the passenger's seat of my car, even though it was closer than hers.

I'd won that battle.

Likely successful only because I'd swept her up in my arms again—ignoring the soft curves of her body, her belly—and just carried her the fifteen feet, opened the door, and set her in the seat.

Likely *that* was successful because she was also still dizzy and not at full force.

Plus, she had a phone call to make.

Now she'd made the call, waited on hold, and then when she began to speak, I struck, taking advantage of her distraction, of her having to listen and respond to buckle her in, to close the door, to round the hood.

I'd folded in, hit the button to turn on my car, and then pulled away from the curb.

All before she could protest...or do something stupid like get out of that seat.

On that note, I checked to make sure the locks were engaged.

Beth was a spitfire. I wouldn't doubt her ability to pull out some ninja skills and leap from the car, completing several full flips before landing on her feet, of course.

Then again, she was dizzy.

Then again, she was pregnant.

"No," she said softly. "It hasn't been this bad before."

A pause, a female voice in the background.

"Yes, a-a friend," she said once that female voice stopped, "is driving me. Yes, I'll do that." Another beat. "Okay, thank you."

I glanced over, saw her hand drop away from her ear, the cell phone's screen showing the call had ended, and I braced, expecting her to tear into me. But she didn't, just turned toward the window and stared out the glass and went completely quiet.

So quiet that I couldn't stand it, couldn't stand hearing the tires rolling over the asphalt, the bumps from the potholes—because city *fucking* roads—and leaned forward, flicking the knob on the radio.

My playlist began sliding through the air, *Black Hole Sun* picking up right in the middle.

Talking about washing away the rain and warmth being gone.

The perfect song for my mood, for my life.

So perfect, so fucking haunting and captivating that I didn't immediately recognize Beth had gone still.

Statue still.

Her gaze still on whatever was on the other side of that glass, but not seeing it now.

No, somewhere inside me, I knew she was captivated by the lyrics, by the haunting voice, by the song that sliced right through my middle.

"You like Soundgarden?" I asked when the song wound down, fading into the background, drifting into Creedence, which was kickass because Creedence always was, but it didn't slice through me in the same way Chris Cornell's voice did.

A jerk, her eyes remaining away from me, and the tone of her voice had me wishing she would turn toward me, toss one of her cocky smiles my way.

"Yeah."

Just *yeah*.

"I thought—" I didn't know why I was still talking. I should be thankful she'd shut up and wasn't giving me any lip.

Her shoulders inched up.

I pressed on. "You'd like Madonna or something."

Silence.

Then, "I do like Madonna and 98 Degrees and the Beatles and Creedence Clearwater Revival," she said, tilting her head toward the radio, though still not looking at me. "And Lizzo and Bieber and Stellar and random bands I find on Spotify who hardly have any streams, but their songs kick butt." A shrug. "I'm a Swiftie, and I dance to J-Lo. But I'm also down for Mötley Crew and Bruce and the Temptations. If it has a beat, I'll shake my ass to it or clap my hands or stomp my feet."

That wasn't the most words she'd ever said at once.

Not to me. Not even in my vicinity.

But it was the most words she'd given me that provided me an insight into her mind.

An insight I didn't want but now had bouncing around my brain anyway.

She liked music.

She liked many different kinds of it.

She...

Was crying.

What the fuck?

I'd stopped at a signal, could see her pale reflection in the window. Which meant I could also see the stark look in her eyes, could see the tears dripping down her cheeks.

And again *what the fuck?*

Slowly, surreptitiously, she lifted a hand, wiping at those tears, and I knew from the sneaky way she'd attempted the maneuver that she didn't want me to know she was crying.

Which was fine with me.

I didn't want to understand that was why her voice had sounded odd as she'd spoken of something innocuous like music. I didn't want to know why she was upset, didn't want to find out it was because I was an asshole, didn't want to discover it was for another reason.

Worry for the babies or for herself. Or maybe just Beth being Beth. Or probably, more likely, it was whatever shit that made women like her cry—a broken nail, her favorite perfume out of stock, her lipstick clashing with her outfit.

A horn blared behind me, and I cursed, hitting the gas, moving forward, lifting a hand in apology to the person behind me.

Which just meant that I got that same person swerving around me, flipping me the bird as they sped by, not giving a fuck that I'd apologized.

Cool.

Moving on.

I was almost to the hospital. Pru and Marcel would be

there, and by the sounds of that phone call she'd just finished, her doctor would be meeting her there, too. She wouldn't be my problem any longer, and I could go home, could enjoy my days off.

I had three of them off in a row, a long weekend that was unusual with the season underway.

Would I be enjoying them by myself? Hopefully.

Was that the way I preferred, even as it was unlikely because my teammates would probably seek me out and try (succeed) to annoy the shit out of me? Yes.

Smothering a sigh, I turned into the driveway of the hospital, pulling up to the front doors, and throwing the transmission into park.

Her shoulders hitched up again when I slid to a stop. "I can walk—"

"We're here," I said, throwing open my door. "You're not walking."

I rounded the hood, got to her side just as she was opening the metal panel, putting her feet down and starting to stand.

"What part of *not walking* don't you understand?"

"What part of *I can walk* don't *you* understand?"

But I was done arguing. I just bent and picked her up again, bringing her into the ER and setting her on one of the chairs at the reception desk when the woman nodded at me.

Beth glared up at me for a beat then turned to the receptionist and handed over her insurance card and ID, letting her know that her doctor had called ahead.

Which meant that was my cue to go.

Which was exactly what I'd intended to do when I left her in that chair and headed out to my car.

But...I didn't see Pru and Marcel on the way out, didn't see their car in the lot when I circled through the rows.

I should have left, pulled right out, and gone back to my empty house.

Beth in that chair.

Alone.

Beth in my car, hiding her tears.

Not alone and yet completely by herself.

Beth—

I parked in an empty spot and, like a goddamned idiot, found myself walking back into that emergency department.

FOUR

Beth

I WAS STARING at my hands, head still spinning, trying not to worry.

The doctor hadn't seemed all that concerned when I had spoken to her on the phone. Her tone had been calm when she'd advised me to come in and get checked out, just to be on the safe side.

But these weren't my babies to take risks with.

The moment I had gotten dizzy I should have been here, just to make sure.

Because I was the vessel carrying extremely precious cargo.

And if I'd done something to harm Pru and Marcel's babies by thinking it wasn't a big deal—

Tears threatened.

A-fucking-gain.

So many tears. *All* the freaking time. Add that to my list of lovely pregnancy side effects that made me an *awesome* catch (yes, that was sarcasm).

I knew the tears, in particular, were because of the hormones and the high stakes of everything, because I was under stress and trying to play this whole pregnancy off like it was no big deal and yet feeling like I was one wrong move away from fucking everything up at every moment.

And I had twenty weeks left. Twenty weeks of worrying and trying to stay calm so I didn't do something stupid and hurt them.

And now I'd passed out in a bar.

A *bar!*

I was pregnant and would have taken a header *in a bar* if not for Raph.

Who'd spent the entire time after I'd collapsed looking at me like I was worse than a bug squished on the bottom of his shoe. After he'd gone full romance hero and stopped me from hitting my head.

Pathetic.

Lusting after him, trying to make him like me, trying to make him *see* me.

No one saw me.

Not really.

"Beth Mason?"

I glanced up from my hands, saw the nurse in the open door, and breathed deep. Then I pushed to my feet, concentrating on putting one in front of the other.

Because the fucking room was spinning.

Because black spots were gathering at the edges of my vision.

"Ms. Mason, are you okay?"

I gripped a chair back, wavering on my feet. "No," I whispered. I wasn't okay. Something was wrong. I couldn't make it across the room. I couldn't. "I'm sorry." Focusing on the nurse, who was moving toward me, I tried desperately to get the room to steady. "I'm sorry," I said again. "I—"

An arm behind my knees, another wrapping around my shoulders.

A warm chest against my side as I was hefted into the air. "I've got her," Raph said, his rasping voice gliding over me.

"Can you bring her this way, sir?" the nurse said. "And then I'll have you step back out into the waiting room."

"I'm her boyfriend."

A pause.

Probably, the nurse was studying Raph's face, trying to decipher that for the lie it was, but he was big and serious, and I knew he could give a brooding look like no other. I'd felt that burn more often than not.

Which was probably why the nurse just murmured, "Follow me."

Then we were moving.

Me. Him. My brain sloshing around my skull and making it very difficult to focus on anything. My eyes staying closed, hoping that when I opened them again the room would be steady and the worry wouldn't be gnawing at me and that this would all just be a lesson in being extra vigilant for naught.

He turned sideways and I knew he was shuffling me through one door then another. Then the lights behind my lids grew brighter, the low hum of noise in the background got louder.

A whoosh.

A soft, "In here."

Then Raph was setting me on a bed.

I took a breath, released it slowly, and opened my eyes.

The nurse was there.

Raph was gone.

Right.

"Oh, my God," Pru exclaimed, moving into the room, her ponytail swinging behind her. "Beth, honey, are you all right?"

Beth.

Not the babies.

That settled somewhere deep in my heart, soothed an ache that only Hazel and Pru could.

They'd been there.

They knew me more deeply than anyone else on the planet.

Of course, that still meant they didn't really know me at all.

I had a whole castle's worth of doors and floors, most of them slammed and locked closed, barred with chains and furniture, and the heavy ones, the ones with the strongest and heaviest chains, the biggest armoires blocking access, were deep in the basement.

No one entered those rooms.

Not me.

Not my friends.

Not any man I'd ever been with.

But Pru's concern settled on the main floor, leaving the demons and darkness untouched in the basement of my mental castle.

"The babies are okay," I said.

The obstetrician on call had just left, wheeling the ultrasound machine away with her. Two babies. Two heartbeats. Placentas okay. The amniotic fluid in both sacs was good. The babies' growth was on target. In fact, they were measuring like singleton babies, rather than on the twin size chart.

So that spoke to my stretch marks...and many more to come.

Pru moved in close, squeezed my hand. "I'm glad." Her free

hand smoothed lightly over my cheek. "And I'm glad you are, too."

This woman was almost unrecognizable to me.

Pru had been so...so self-contained...until the man who walked in behind her had entered Pru's life. There was concern in Marcel's pretty eyes, and his big body dwarfed Pru's—even though I was no shrinking violet myself—considering that I'd played hockey for years and had the strength and body time to show it.

No wonder the babies were measuring big.

Between Marcel and Pru, I was cooking two future hockey players.

"Beth."

I glanced over Pru's shoulder, met Marcel's gaze. "You good?" he asked.

"The babies are fine," I whispered, my eyes sliding down to the bed.

"Beth," he said again.

My gaze slid back.

"You good?" A slight emphasis on *you* that warmed me in almost the same way that Pru's concern had, reminding me that Marcel had become dear to me, that he'd been making a home for himself on the ground floor of my life, that he was important.

I nodded. "I'm good."

Pru squeezed my hand again.

"I'm sorry to scare you." A breath, trying to speak through the sharp strikes of guilt. "The doctor says my blood pressure is low, and that's why I've been dizzy. I just need to take it easy, drink more water, and ditch my tight clothes so the babies are getting enough blood and nothing is cutting off my circulation." I forced a smile. "Not that I'd be wearing them much longer anyway." A pat to my rounded stomach. "Not with this belly growing more by the day."

"You love your skirts," Pru said softly.

I did.

And my heels.

But those were out, too. Unsteady feet and legs didn't need me to be on four-inch heels.

"The plus is I get to go shopping." Now my smile wasn't forced. "Which, as you know, is one of my favorite things."

Pru grinned. "I'll hold your purse while you're in the dressing room."

I clutched my hands to my chest, fluttered my lashes. "Like a true best friend."

"Surviving torture?" Pru teased.

"Picking out kickass outfits for her favorite wingwoman."

Another squeeze. "That, too."

I covered my hand then peeled it gently away. "It's late," I said. "I know Marcel is off tomorrow, but you've got to get ready for your trip. You should go to bed."

"I'm staying." No argument, no discussion.

Not that I would expect anything different from my friend.

She was a badass, an adventure seeker, but beneath all of that was a big heart who loved deeply.

Pru was also a scout for the Breakers, the same team that Marcel played for, but their schedules didn't always align. She was leaving early in the morning and would be gone a week then would return and work with the rest of the Player Development department to keep an eye on the young up-and-coming players they might one day draft and those currently under contract but not yet playing in the big leagues.

Marcel was a forward, one of the best on the Breakers.

He'd be in town, working hard, recovering from the brutalness of the game itself, staying fit and strong for the rest of the long season. The Breakers were about halfway through, and as I had learned in my year here, the toughest stretch of the season was still ahead of them. Soon the work would really get going, the team buckling down for play-offs, trying to win every game, to get every point so they would have a good berth going into the post-season.

See?

I might live in tight skirts and high heels, never go anywhere without my lipstick and have worked for charities and not for professional sports teams, but I was smart, I learned, and my most recent job up in New York had been for an organization that connected underprivileged kids with sports opportunities—equipment, coaching, leagues, travel fees for tournaments they wouldn't otherwise be able to attend. Plus, I was friends with Pru, had been to more than my fair share of games over the years.

So, despite not being a sports fan, I knew plenty about hockey.

Which was why I knew that my friend needed to go home so that she could be fresh for her job.

"You should go get some sleep"—I glanced at Marcel—"*both* of you. Sleepless nights will be coming soon enough. You might as well—"

Pru scowled. "We're staying."

"I'm—"

"*We're staying.*"

This time from Marcel, Pru nodding her agreement.

And I looked at my friend's face, at Marcel's, and I was too tired to argue further.

So I just nodded.

Locked away how that made me feel in one of those rooms on the ground floor.

To keep it safe.

FIVE

Raph

I'D STOOD in the hall until Pru and Marcel showed up, watching from a distance, slipping out when Marcel had texted, saying they were in the waiting room.

I'd gotten them in, then left, walking out the sliding glass doors and into the night air.

All while ignoring the look that the nurse who'd eyed me while I'd carried Beth in gave me. Probably thinking I was a total asshole because I'd said I was her boyfriend but had promptly left Beth to her own devices in that patient room, and now I was leaving.

I already knew I was an asshole.

I'd made a pregnant woman cry—or at the very least, I'd added to her stress with all my yelling.

After she'd passed out, and when she was carrying my close friends' twins.

Not getting paid for it. Not doing it for any other reason

except that her friend and her friend's man dreamed of having babies.

Giving up her body.

Her life.

Her fun.

And I'd made her cry.

Because I'd yelled.

Christ. I fucking *hated* that. My dad had been a yeller. I'd had plenty of coaches over the years who'd seemingly made it their life's work to scream at their players.

I didn't like it.

I *took* it because most of the time that was the way of my world.

I'd found a way to use that screaming and yelling, to internalize it and find the motivation in it.

But *I* didn't yell.

I didn't yell because the volume, the tone, the screaming always sent ice through my spine, froze every nerve. An instant —and thankfully, because I'd worked on it—short reaction. I bounced back, could focus it, could find that motivation...but I always *always* had that first reaction.

And I'd promised myself I would never *ever* be that guy.

Tonight...I'd been that guy.

"Fuck," I hissed, fingers clenching the door handle of my car so fucking tight that it was a goddamned miracle I didn't dent it or rip it clear off as I yanked it open.

But my car stayed in one piece as I dropped into the driver's seat, jabbed at the button to start the ignition.

I should have hit the gas, got the fuck back to my empty house.

Forget the night.

Forget all the shit about spending time with Beth, how her smiles and conversation had made me feel, all the shit that just *being* with her and my subsequent acting like an asshole had dredged up.

Instead, I sat in my car, my gaze locked on the sliding glass doors, and waited.

For Marcel to come out.

For Marcel to pull the car around.

For Beth to be wheeled out in a chair, right up to the passenger's side door. For Pru to help her into the seat, something that ended up with me clenching something else—the steering wheel this time so I didn't go over and help her get Beth safely into the car.

For the door to shut.

For Marcel to pull away.

And stupidly, I put my car into gear and followed Marcel. All the way to Beth's house.

THE TRIO HAD GONE INSIDE.

A long time later, Pru and Marcel came out, moving to their car, Marcel's arm around Pru's shoulders, keeping her close to my body.

They both looked exhausted and worried.

"Fuck," I muttered, their expressions not helping to ease that knot in my stomach.

But they were leaving, so I knew that Beth must be okay.

Otherwise they would still be inside that house.

Logically, I understood that.

Inside, that knot hadn't gone away.

So I sat in my dark car, waited until they'd walked away, and then I went up to the hide-a-key—the location of which I knew because I'd gone with Marcel to feed Beth's cat when she, Pru, and Hazel had gone on a girl's weekend. I didn't think about the fact that Monica had never been interested in spending time with Pru, Hazel, or the other guys' girls, even though she'd been invited. Nor did I think about the bitching she'd given me when I'd encouraged her to go and she hadn't had fun. I didn't think about any of that, or Monica, even, or the other women close to the team and their various activities as I extracted the key.

I was focused on that knot in my gut.

I was thinking about Beth's reflection in the window and the tears on her cheeks.

I was locked on how scared she'd looked in that hospital bed, her expression completely unguarded because she'd thought she'd been alone. I was fixed on how her expression had then become guarded, exuding faux calm went the nurse and doctor had bustled in.

Then became vulnerable again after they'd left.

Beth didn't do vulnerable.

She was big old brass balls and red lipstick. Tall ass heels and tight skirts.

She was...sleeping on her side on her big purple suede couch, a blanket over her, hands tucked up under her face.

Soft.

So fucking beautiful she was nearly angelic.

Her breathing was slow and steady. I saw that Pru and Marcel had put everything within arm's reach—water, snacks, e-reader, TV remote, laptop, and all their respective chargers. They'd even cleared a path to the bathroom, rearranging the furniture so Beth could always have a hand on something if she needed to make her way while no one was with her.

I should have gone then.

She was asleep and settled, made safe by her friends.

But...no one was with her.

I got that it was probably her own doing, that she was stubborn and wouldn't want her friends to worry.

But...*no one* was with her.

So instead of moving quietly out her front door, replacing the key in that dumb fake rock outside, I moved to the big purple armchair and sank down.

And then I watched Beth sleep.

With one eye open, on full alert for any bit of movement, of distress on her part.

And then, eventually, with both eyes closed as exhaustion overtook me.

A GROAN.

A gasp.

A moan.

I frowned, started to roll over in bed, and then realized I wasn't lying down. I was sitting up, my neck stiff and aching.

And I was in Beth's house.

Early morning light was filtering in through the windows.

Minus sleeping upright, the ugly-ass purple chair was comfortable, and it actually fit me, which was a rarity. Usually, I set my ass on a chair and hoped the spindly fucker didn't collapse. So I certainly hadn't expected a suede purple chair to be anything but a lesson in feminine discomfort.

Bitter?

Fuck yeah, I was.

But when I had a mom like I'd had, when I'd been with the women I had...

Feminine discomfort was a common experience.

My eyes flew open when I heard another moan.

Only this time it was a moaned-out word. A moaned-out, "*No.*"

Spine going stiff, I shot up to my feet.

Beth's brows were drawn sharply together, her eyes still closed, shifting uncomfortably on the couch, head digging into her pillow. Dreaming.

A bad one.

"No!"

Not a moan this time, but a yell, and not the kind that had me finding the motivation on the ice or in the weight room. This yell had every *single* one of my nerves freezing as I shoved out of the chair.

"No." Quieter now, her head shifting from side to side. "No, don't hurt her. Don't touch her. *No!*"

The last was ear-piercing, making me jump.

"Fuck," I whispered.

Nightmare or memory, I didn't know.

What I *did* know?

That I wasn't going to stand there like an idiot and watch the fear in her mind etch itself onto her face, wasn't going to listen to her groaning and gasping and telling some fucking monster in her brain *no.*

So I moved to her side, knelt on the carpet, and reached for her.

SIX

Beth

I WAS in the corner of the room.

Plush carpet beneath my bottom, silk on my body.

The air conditioning was pumping in the house, like it always did, summer or winter or in between, and since I wasn't under the thick, down comforter my mom had picked out for my bed, I was shivering.

But it wasn't just the air conditioning that had me shivering.

He was hurting her.

Again.

The *thunks* were familiar, and they always meant that my mom walked carefully the next day, winced when she went up the stairs, and I had to be really *really* gentle if I hugged her.

And I was in the corner of the room, hiding behind my five-story dollhouse, being quiet.

Like my mom had said to do.

Because I always listened to my mom.

Always.

But that night the *thunks* were louder than normal. That night my mom, who normally was silent, began crying out.

And...I couldn't take it.

So I stood up and stepped out of that shadowed corner, goose bumps spreading on my skin as the air-conditioned air moved over my body.

But the *thunks* weren't stopping.

And I could hear my mom crying out, louder with each whoosh of noise.

My bare toes sank into the carpet as I walked across the room, reached for the knob. My fingers slipped on the cool metal, trying to turn it, but eventually, I managed to get it open and moved into the hall.

The noise was louder there.

But I didn't go back into my room. Because my mom was nice, so much nicer than my stepdad.

We'd made cookies that afternoon, with extra chocolate chips, and my mom had even let me eat some of the dough before it was cooked.

Even though my stepdad said sweets made little girls fat.

I had liked the cookies even better than the dough, but I'd liked making them with my mom even more.

So I needed to make the *thunks* stop.

So I walked down the hall, reached for the handle of my mom and stepdad's room.

Turned it and—

GASPING, I sat upright, the memories choking me...like those hands had done that night.

"Baby." Warm palms on my arms, fingers wrapping

securely and holding me in place when I would have bolted, and I was so entrenched in the past that it took me several long moments to realize that the hands were gentle.

Not squeezing.

Not bruising.

Not hurting.

Just lightly running up and down my arms.

And paired with a gentle voice.

"Baby, wake up. You're okay. You're safe." *Raph's* voice. "Beth, honey. Sugarpie, you're good, sweetie. You're okay."

Eyes flashing open, I saw that I wasn't hallucinating.

Having nightmares, yes. But not hallucinating.

I was in my house, on my couch. The setup Pru and Marcel had left me with still in place.

And Raph was there.

In *my* house.

Kneeling in front of *my* couch.

Putting his hands on *my* body.

"What are you doing here?" I whispered.

"You're safe," he said again, still in that gentle voice.

That wasn't what I'd asked.

"What are you doing *here*?" I repeated.

His eyes were pools of deep blue ocean water, hiding mysteries and secrets and a man who was as scary as he was interesting. I wanted to know all of those depths, ferret out the enigma that was beneath. I wanted to heal the breach in him, to make him understand that not all women were bad, but I wasn't going to do it.

Because I didn't want it enough to reveal my own secrets in the process.

And to have an actual relationship built on trust and mutual respect and love, sharing secrets was kind of par for the course—or puck for the net, or whatever.

"You need to go," I whispered when the silence between us had stretched long enough so that I knew he wasn't going to answer.

"You dizzy?" he asked instead of moving, his warm hands still on my arms.

A beat. "No."

His eyes narrowed, studying me closely.

"You need to go," I said again.

"You hungry?"

Not only not going to answer me about why he was in my house, but also not going to listen to me about leaving.

Fucking *great*.

And yet, I was also trying to ignore the little tingle inside me, the one that liked that he was there in my house. The idiotic tingle that liked his deep, mysterious eyes on mine, relished in his touch, was jumping with joy and throwing a total *told-you-so* my way, considering I'd been playing with fire for the better part of three years trying to get his attention.

Now I had it.

And I couldn't decide if I was terrified or really freaking excited.

Both. None. All of that and more.

Which was why I whispered, "You need to go," for a third time.

Which he ignored. For a third time.

But then he stood up, and I thought that perhaps, for one second, he was going to listen to me.

I should have known better.

Because instead of marching to my front door (and out it, preferably), he moved into my kitchen.

"What is going on?" I muttered under my breath, the sentiment seemingly asked twice over when the sound of pots and pans rattling, my fridge opening and closing met my ears.

My cell rang just as I heard the *click-click-click* of my stove lighting.

What. The. *Fuck?*

Eyes drifting from the kitchen to my cell's screen, I saw that Pru was calling—probably from the airport, probably worried, probably hating that I had forced her to go home the night before.

So I didn't delay in answering my phone.

"Hey," I said.

"You okay?"

"I'm fine," I said. "Not dizzy at all this morning." Not after my head had cleared because Raph had put his hands on me, rubbed gently up and down my arms, had used those soft words, that gentle tone with me.

Of course, I hadn't tried to stand up either, so that might be a game changer.

But, truthfully, I *did* feel better.

Hopefully, it would be like the doctor said, here temporarily and passing like the wind—or passing like the brief moments of Raph pretending to give a shit about me.

The dizziness would be here again, gone tomorrow.

"You sure?" Pru asked. "I can—"

"Honey. We're fine. If something comes up, which it won't because I'll take it easy and follow the doctor's advice and drink seven million gallons of water and retire my tight clothes and eat more—though that's something I'm not even sure is possible —but if it does come back, I'll call Marcel and the doctor, and then I'll let you know."

Quiet in my ear. Then, "If something happens to you because of me—"

"I'm healthy," I whispered. "*They're* healthy, and I'll keep you posted every step of the way. Remember, babe, I *wanted* to do this for you." I'd wanted to do something good for my friend, something that would wash away the cloying stench that seemed impossible for me to rid myself of. "I'm *okay*. I know it's hard because this isn't your body, but don't doubt for one minute that I'm treating these babies like the precious cargo they are."

"That was never in doubt, Bethie."

Warmth sliding along cold tile floors, seeping under the bottom of a closed door. "Thanks, honey," I whispered. "Now, try not to worry, and know I'll send you and Marcel a bajillion texts today."

"A bajillion?" Pru asked lightly.

"How about a bajillion and one?"

Laughter in my friend's tone. "That's better."

"Good. Now have fun scouting the players," I said, a la *The Princess Bride* and my favorite line from it ("*Have fun storming the castle.*").

Pru chuckled and said her goodbyes.

And just for good measure, I immediately sent a text to her and Marcel.

> Baby update 1024 We're comfortably sequestered on the couch.

Pru replied,

> Love you, Bethie.

Marcel, man of few words, just sent a thumb's up.

Quiet. Effective.

A *plunk* in front of me.

My gaze shot up from my phone screen, saw that Raph had emerged from the kitchen, a scraper in one hand. The other was empty, having presumably carried the large cup of water recently plunked onto the table Pru had dragged over the night before.

"Drink," *my* man of few words ordered before disappearing back into the kitchen.

Not *my* man, I thought, watching him walk, studying the heavy muscles of his legs, the lean strength of his shoulders and waist. Big and tall and strong, but not a behemoth like Smitty, who played defense and could battle along the boards with the toughest in the league. His strength hid a huge, soft heart (that had been wrapped up and passed over to the woman he loved, Kailey, on a puck-colored platter).

That wasn't Raph.

His heart was buried deep, protected with spikes and armor and a whole forest of cat-o-nines.

Also, he wasn't *mine*, wouldn't ever be.

Biting back a sigh, I glanced down at the glass of water, condensation gathering on its outside, and I picked it up, drank deeply.

Drank and drank until the entire glass was empty.

For Pru.

For Marcel.

For the babies in my belly.

For...well, I couldn't ignore the niggling feeling that perhaps a small part of me drank it for herself.

SEVEN

Raph

EGGS AND TOAST.

And water.

It wasn't fucking gourmet, but if it stopped her from feeling dizzy, prevented her from passing out and hurting herself or those babies...

Well, I was scrambling eggs and juggling toast into her toaster.

That was answer enough, and the why of that answer—the *why* of why I was doing this, sticking my nose in her business, sleeping in a fucking chair beside her, cooking breakfast—was something I wasn't going to focus on.

Doing, not thinking.

I'd done too much thinking already.

And those tears, that nightmare...I *couldn't* fucking think about it.

So I was grating cheese into a pan, turning the eggs gently

with a spatula, adding pepper (salt would wait until the end, just like my mom had taught me), and listening for the toast to pop up.

When it did, I buttered it, slathered strawberry jam (the only variety in her fridge and I approved) on top of both slices, scooped the eggs out of the pan, and then carried the plate to Beth in the family room.

The glass was empty, so I set the plate down, grabbed the glass, went back for the fork and napkin, refilled her water, and carried all three back toward her.

The plate was untouched.

No surprise, since I had the fork in my hand.

I pressed it into hers, draped the napkin over her lap, and said, "Eat. Drink."

Blue, blue eyes on mine. I expected them to spark fire—she wasn't the type of woman to take orders, even *if* she was off her game.

But there wasn't a single spark in those cerulean irises.

Not one.

She just bent her head, forked up some eggs, and ate.

Fuck.

I should be thankful she was quiet, not shoveling out sass for once. But...it was wrong. Beth shouldn't be quiet, and she shouldn't be passing out, and she shouldn't have fucking night-mares where she was crying out to someone not to hurt her, not to touch her.

Fuck.

"Beth," I said, and she paused, the fork almost at her lips. "Honey, I—"

My words stuck in my throat when she glanced up.

Empty. Desolate. A wide expanse of barren ice. A frigid dessert.

No red lipstick. No pinked cheeks.

A pale face, empty eyes, and...

I didn't want to think about how much I hated that, so I just said, "Eat," and then I got up and moved back into the kitchen, taking care of the pan, wiping down the counters. By the time I circled back with a third glass of water, Beth had finished her plate.

She looked at the refilled glass, up to me, and fuck me, but I was damned glad to see that her lips twitched, her eyes weren't the frosty wasteland.

Amusement had coiled through, sunshine melting ice, cracking through the layers of frost.

"I don't think the doctor meant to drink so much water that I'm going to pass out because my ass is waddling to the bathroom every five minutes."

I bit back a grin.

"And that would be down from every ten minutes since these babies already seem to enjoy tap-dancing on my bladder."

"You can feel them?" I asked softly.

It was a question that revealed too much.

"Yeah," she whispered. "They move a lot, and they really like that jam. See?" She lifted the edge of her shirt, exposing her rounded belly, and I watched, watched in a way that stole every bit of air from my lungs as her stomach bounced and twitched.

That was...

My arm moved before I processed it, hand sliding across the space, lifting toward her stomach. It was too far, too much. I didn't have permission to touch her, let alone her belly, but I ran my fingers over it anyway.

I felt that flutter.

I—*fuck—felt that flutter.*

Butterfly wings on my fingertips. Like a twitching muscle. And then a soft push that had me jerking my hand back, jumping to my feet.

"Drink," I rasped.

"Raph," she whispered, dropping her shirt, blue eyes not sparking, her skin still pale, especially minus her red lips. But there was understanding written into the lines of her face.

And...

I needed to go.

"Drink," I said again.

"Okay, Raph," she said, voice as soft as velvet.

Good.

That was good.

That was...all I could take.

I turned and walked out the door.

It was early enough that the cool air had partially fogged the glass ringing the boards.

Which was just as well.

I wanted the privacy, the quiet.

Which wasn't just as well.

Considering I got it for all of fifteen minutes before Smitty hauled my big ass onto the ice, feet in skates, legs in sweats, gloves on, and long ass stick in my hands, smirk on my face.

"Self-medicating with ice time?" he boomed.

Yup.

Boomed.

Because Smitty might be a gentle giant, but he had one volume, and that volume was *loud*.

I bit back a sigh, turned, and went back to my shot, wailing on the puck, hearing the *tink* of the goalpost.

Fucking hell.

I'd been aiming for the upper left corner.

No goalie. No pressure. Not even a shooter-tutor.

Just me and my fucked-up head.

Well, and Smitty, who miraculously didn't comment on the fucked-up shot.

"Heads up," he called instead, whipping a puck at me. I took the opportunity and one-timed it, this time thankfully hitting the corner I aimed for.

"Again," Smitty called before that puck hit the ice, winging another my way.

I shot, hit that same corner again, just for good measure.

"Bottom corner now," he said, shagging down a puck and firing it at me.

I shot.

I hit that corner.

And then it was on, Smitty and I playing our casual game of Hockey Horse, moving around the zone, hitting the various spots, trying for various shots—or I was, anyway, considering that Smitty had apparently made it his job to be my puck bitch. Pretty soon my lungs were screaming, my arms were tired, and I was struggling to hit the shots.

Which meant it was no surprise that Smitty called, "Last one, top third of the net on the left.

My favorite place to shoot.

Often open if a goalie had gone down to make a save, and if it wasn't, typically it beaned them right in the helmet.

So if not a goal, then a smack to the goalie.

Win-win, especially with how I'd been feeling the last year.

I swung, followed through, hit that top third of the net.

"Nice," Smitty muttered, skating up beside me, smacking me on the shoulder with that typical Smitty strength, one that nearly had my skate blades jammed down through the ice and into the sand beneath.

I braced, knowing my friend and teammate was a nosy fuck, knowing that he'd want to know why I was out here this morning.

And I didn't want to talk about it, about last night or Beth's rounded belly and how it felt to feel the babies inside move, what it had done to my own heart, how it had ripped my shields clear away and I'd *felt* it, yearned for it. I didn't want to talk about the worry gnawing at the back of my mind, that she wasn't drinking enough or eating enough or that she was dizzy and alone or that she'd fallen back asleep and was having fucking nightmares that had her yelling and begging someone not to touch her.

Her.

Not Beth.

But another *her.*

And that killed me.

Because I wanted to know.

So all of that was swirling, and my arms were tired, and my lungs were on fire, and Smitty was close, the nosy mother-fucker, and one wrong word and that nosy motherfucker would unleash the full force of the gossip train on me.

And I needed that like I needed a hole in my head.

But the gossip train was a train for a reason—once it was trucking along the tracks, it was nearly impossible to get it to stop.

So I was braced, standing on the tracks, prepared to be flattened.

I was tense, knowing it was bearing down on me.

I was...shocked to shit when Smitty clapped me on the shoulder again and didn't ask. Instead, the only thing my team-mate said was, "Pancakes."

Syrup and carbs and a shit-ton of butter.

Yeah, I could go for that. "You making them or are we going to Donna's?"

"Not even a fucking decision, man," Smitty said, clapping me on the shoulder again.

I smiled for the first time in what felt like forever.

"We're going to Donna's."

EIGHT

Beth

TRUTHFULLY, I'd sat on the couch after Raph left, the memories still tightly clutching at my brain, mixing with the way Raph's face had looked when he'd touched me, how it had felt for him to carry me into the hospital, to his car, what it meant that he'd cooked for me, and I'd cried.

Truthfully, I would have liked to pretend it was pregnancy hormones.

But as I curled up on the couch, staring at the full cup of water, I knew it wasn't hormones.

It was the memories.

It was Raph.

So it took me a long time to lose it, to cry out all the shit twisted inside, to let loose all that pressure so the doors would lock tight again.

Then it took me a long time to summon up the energy to get off the couch and get on with my day.

I drank the water first.

Then I moved into my downstairs bathroom, where Pru had moved all of my makeup and face stuff—cleanser, age-defying creams and lotions, moisturizer, serum, and primer—so I did my thing, taking my time and doing it slowly, making sure I'd hidden every trace of my freak-out beneath the concealer and foundation.

And I knew that it would be hidden.

Because I had lots of practice at it.

I'd shed so many tears in my life that I could fill the Hoover Dam.

I just did it silently, on my couch or in my bed or—my favorite—in the shower. Easy to wash away, easy to explain the pinkened skin.

Of course, it would be easier if I didn't cry so much, if I could be one of those women for whom their nightmares tempered their spines, forged them into steel. But I wasn't strong like that. I had a whole fucking castle worth of demons, locked behind doors, with only a few people allowed inside, and fewer of those allowed in just a couple of rooms on the first floor.

Because those spaces were bright and had a lot of windows and pretty decorations and tons of candelabras to scare away the shadows.

Any demons that might show in those rooms were baby-sized.

Ones easily shared and excised.

Ones that made me relatable.

Ones that I could tuck away without effort.

Because the rooms I allowed Hazel and Pru into weren't the basement or the attic or the shadowy little eaves where blackness seemed to cling. I could share them, could rid myself of them.

The rest, the ones with the big, gaping maws, the sharp

teeth and claws, the power to frighten me so thoroughly that I'd crash to my knees, beg them to leave me alone...I attempted to keep them locked away.

So when I cried, it wasn't about the baby demons. My tears were for the biggest ones, those straining at the chains, threatening to break free and ravage, leaving only waste and destruction in their wake.

My makeup hid that.

Expertly contoured cheeks and nose, forehead and jaw, fake lashes every day, perfectly applied liner that had taken me an age to learn how to get just right. Cream shadows with just a hint of glimmer. Brows filled in to frame my eyes. Lips painted my typical bright red.

To hide.

To make sure no one had a reason to find fault, to look deeper, to get angry about.

A perfect representation of everything I was supposed to be.

My clothes completed that image.

They were flattering and sexy, but not too much.

Because if she looked perfect, he would leave her alone, wouldn't notice her, wouldn't *hit* her. Because if I do the same, I'll be safe too.

"Enough," I whispered.

But I couldn't stop myself from studying my reflection, from adding just a tiny bit more blush, one more coat of mascara.

Then I moved back into my family room, to that table Pru and Marcel had set up for me, gaze locking on the empty glass, and before I headed into the spare bedroom where Pru had also moved some clothes and shoes so that I wouldn't have to risk the stairs, just in case, I went back into the kitchen, filled the glass, and drank it down.

I was so going to have to pee every five minutes.

But at least I was upright.

FOR A NON-FASHIONISTA, Pru had done a good job.

My friend was the least girlie of our trio, eschewing dresses and heels for sneakers, sweats, and T-shirts, but she'd pulled together some Beth-level outfits, even minus all the tight.

Of course, tight was relative.

Because even my period pants were tight on my belly, and my normal shirts made boobalicious seem conservative.

All of which was a problem.

Because my period pants were my biggest pants, which meant that shopping was going to need to commence, and it was going to have to commence today.

Oh, the humanity.

Lips twitching, I moved hangers until I found something that would do.

I had one pair of maternity leggings and I could pair that with my blue sweater that spent the majority of its time slipping off one shoulder. I had to be careful with blues sometimes, between my skin tone—olive—and my hair—a bright red that had settled into an auburn over the years—but this shade was perfect, and I loved its slouchy, cozy feel.

Normally, though, I reserved it for days in.

Today, it would have to do for a shopping extravaganza.

And—I turned, studied the shoes on the bed—I'd wear it with my chunky boots.

No heel to trip on, still cute enough that I'd have my shield and, hell, I *liked* them, so I was going to wear them.

So...Pru had done good.

Smiling, I made a mental note to tell my friend she passed the Beth Mason outfit selecting test.

But now I needed to shop, and then when I came home from that, I would bust out my computer, get my work done, and I would make sure all the doors in my mental castle were locked.

Firmly.

With extra chains.

On that thought, I shimmied into my leggings, that slouchy sweater, snagged the boots from the bed and moved back to the couch, sitting down and moving carefully to slip them on.

But I wasn't dizzy, hadn't been from the moment I'd woken up and started chugging water.

No, from the moment I'd sat up and stared into beautiful blue eyes.

Warm blue eyes, like a spring morning, the sun shining down, hands on my arms, face close, and none of the prickly, angry *yelling*.

Just Raph.

And that glimpse of beauty had taken my breath away.

I'd only seen it a few times, and all of those times had come before he'd been with Monica...before things had *ended* with Monica.

Once at CeCe's. I'd been outrageous then in a way that would have made my stepfather lose his shit, but since I'd been out of New York and with my friends and they always got a kick out of me being outrageous, I'd been going full tilt.

Another sort of mask, I supposed.

Another way to hide.

If I could be fun and loud and make them laugh, then they wouldn't see through, they wouldn't notice all the doors that were blocked off.

But that night, I'd made an outrageous joke on the heels of

many other outrageous jokes, and Hazel and Oliver and Pru and Marcel and Smitty had been cracking up. Even Jules, our favorite server, had dropped her tray onto the table and bowed her head, her shoulders rocking with laughter. And Raph...he'd laughed.

It was masculine and strong and intense, and I'd fucking *loved* it.

That glimpse of warm blue eyes.

The turning up of his lips.

The way he'd *looked* at me.

Another time, I'd watched that light fill his face when he'd looked through the glass at a little girl who was cheering raucously for the team.

One final time when I'd been over at Hazel and Oliver's place, after Oliver's career-ending injury. It hadn't been easy on Hazel's man to lose his leg, to lose his career, but in doing so, he'd come full circle, and he'd found Hazel.

And we'd all been eating dinner, just pizza and beer, and sitting around watching a crappy action movie, and Hazel had said something...something that I didn't remember, probably something sweet because that was Hazel, and I remembered watching Oliver's face change, soften in a way it only did for her. Then he had leaned in and gently cupped her cheek.

I hadn't been able to take that gentle, that sweet.

It had been a battering ram to my castle's gates.

To ease the burn I'd turned away...and had seen Raph's expression.

And...it had been so beautiful that it had awakened something in me that was absolutely terrifying.

Need.

Desperation to see that look again.

"Enough."

And *God,* it was enough. Being in my mind, my memories, my past was *enough.*

I stood, grabbed my purse, and battened down the house.

Then I took a Lyft to CeCe's, picked up my car, and went shopping.

Alone.

Right.

NINE

Raph

WE WERE four big hockey players crammed into a tiny ass eighties-style oak booth, flower curtains on the window behind our heads separating the booths.

Our drinks were sitting on doilies.

Actual doilies.

Coffee for me and Cas. Water and coffee for Smitty and Theo.

And we were impatiently waiting for our pancakes.

My day was looking up, mostly because Smitty was talking about his woman, Kailey, who was Smitty's polar opposite (smart and shy and soft, but perfect for Smitty). But because with Smitty prattling on about Kailey—his favorite subject— that meant he wasn't picking at me for being on the ice early on a day we didn't *have* to be on the ice, not trying to get in my head and send that gossip train barreling down the tracks toward me.

Instead, Theo and Cas had been in the weight room, and

mention of Donna's had sent the weights right back onto the rack, and they'd horned in on pancakes.

Fine with me.

Plenty of pancakes at Donna's.

A buffer from Smitty and his gossip-attuned antenna.

Though I could have done without being pressed thigh-to-thigh to Theo.

I'd rather be pressed to Beth.

Which was a problem in and of itself.

Especially since instead of choosing my typical Nutella-filled flapjacks, I'd ordered strawberry.

Fuck.

I *was* fucked.

But I was pretending I wasn't, pretending it was normal for me to have ordered strawberry pancakes when Smitty and I had eaten here enough together for my teammate to know that I only *ever* got Nutella ones.

Which was why I'd done my best to get my friend on the Kailey ramble—not hard since Smitty loved his girl—and was silently drinking my coffee, doily or not, as it rolled on.

But pondering the doilies, the flower-laden curtains, the scarred Formica tables, and the fact that half of my ass was hanging out of the booth didn't mean my mind was so busy to not have missed Beth walking into the restaurant.

The flash of red drew my eyes to the right.

Pretty auburn hair.

Not fire engine red, but softer with hints of brown.

Like I said, pretty, and the first thing I'd noticed about her.

The second being those bright red lips, currently curved up in a smile at the young hostess leading her to a booth perpendicular to where the boys and I were sitting.

My stomach began churning, and I tried not to turn my head.

Tried and failed because I watched that smiling Beth in a pretty blue sweater that matched her eyes, her legs in tight black pants that had my temper spiking because they were tight and hell because they showed off her shapely thighs, the lush bottom curve of her ass. Her feet were in—thank fuck for one tiny victory—low-heeled boots.

Fuck, she was pretty.

That had my temper spiking.

I didn't want to notice that either.

I didn't want to notice one fucking thing about her, and instead, I was tracking every step, watching her move in that fluid way, even though she was carrying two babies, holding my breath until she made it into the booth, her ass sliding across the unpadded oak bench.

Unpadded, I knew, because my ass was on my own unpadded bench.

One that wasn't particularly comfortable.

One that had me getting up and moving to the hostess stand, asking her to bring Beth one of the few cushions Donna's had available on request.

My own ass was hardened from years of bruising it on the ice.

Beth's was lush and curvy and...

Fuck, but I didn't want her to be uncomfortable.

"So, she came up to me after she got out of the bathroom," Cas was saying as I returned to the table, studiously avoiding both Smitty's gaze *and* that booth perpendicular to ours, even though I was watching out of the corner of my eye to make sure that the hostess brought over the cushion. Thankfully, the conversation had turned to Cas, and Cas being young and hot and a professional athlete, had no shortage of crazy stories, most of them involving women and stupidity and most of that was because he continued to go to bars where young, beautiful, but perhaps not the most mature, women spent a good deal of time.

Hot, no doubt.

But a fucking nightmare, as I had personally lived through.

"And she was fucking pissed as hell because I'd talked to Jules." He tossed up his hands. "That I *talked* to our waitress like a fucking human being. I don't know what her deal was, but it was like she expected me to either be a total dick to Jules or to communicate in sign language or smoke signals or something that didn't involve me actually verbally addressing her. Like my voice was somehow going to make Jules strip down and fuck me right on my stool."

"Jules?" Theo groaned. "Aw fuck, man, please tell me that you didn't take that chick to CeCe's."

Cas winced. "We'd been on three dates," I muttered. "I thought she was at least *semi* normal."

"Rookie mistake." Smitty shook his head, lifted his mug, and took a sip. "We fly under the radar at CeCe's because the staff and patrons are cool. We can't do that if you start bringing women there who can't deal."

Like Monica.

Though Smitty didn't say that.

Lucky for me, Monica had hated it so much she wasn't going to stalk the place hoping for me to show back up. Nope, she'd just broken into my apartment and tried to convince me that she really *did* want a baby and she'd just made a mistake.

I'd had to make it clear, *really* fucking clear, that we were done.

A-fucking-gain.

Which hadn't made me happy.

Though, thank fuck, that meant she'd cleared out, I'd changed the locks, and all was good again.

Good being a relative term, I supposed.

"Like I said," Cas muttered. "I thought she was cool. Unfortunately—or maybe fortunately, all things considered—she proved quickly she wasn't." He sighed. "And I made it worth Jules's while. She got a huge ass tip for putting up with Chelsea's bullshit."

"And she might have to put up Chelsea's bullshit again if your *semi-normal date* decides to stakeout CeCe's," Smitty pointed out, protective to my core, particularly of women and particularly of women like Julie, who worked hard to provide for her son at home and didn't need bullshit from a puck bunny who couldn't even stand for her date to talk to a waitress.

Cas winced again. "Fuck."

"Yeah," Smitty said on a sigh. "Fuck." I plunked my mug down. "You need to check in with Jules, make sure she doesn't get any blowback from your rejects."

Said casually.

But in a way that had me eyeing my friend closely.

Said *too* casually.

I studied Smitty's face, saw interference and interest brewing in the edges of his eyes. Nosy, pushy, matchmaking motherfucker.

But thankfully that gaze was directed at Cas, not me.

So that was a victory. For the moment, anyway.

"Fuck," Cas said. "I'll make sure she's good."

Smitty nodded. "Good." Then the big gossiping bastard turned his focus to me. "Just like you're making sure that Be—"

"Here you go boys!" the waitress—a hundred years old if she was a day—chirped, our plates stacked up her arms.

Pancakes.

Bacon.

Eggs.

Toast for Theo, who'd for some reason decided he needed more carbs.

For my part, I was ready to kiss our waitress, but I settled for passing out plates and getting everyone settled, encouraging them to dig in to their food so their mouths were full, and they could focus on something that wasn't me.

Wasn't Smitty putting the pieces together of me and Beth.

Wasn't Smitty commenting on those pieces.

And then I started shoving pancakes into *my* mouth.

So *it* was full, and no responses could possibly be required.

TEN

Beth

THE NICE COLLEGE-AGE girl brought me a cushion, which was sweet, I thought, and probably solely a byproduct of the fact that I'd finally popped.

Not just fat, but definitely preggers.

Which was...interesting.

I'd had my first person touching my belly—unwanted and unwarranted—on the way to pancakes, after having parked my car in the lot at Donna's. I'd been on my way to the outlets, always loving to search the racks for a great deal, but as I'd gotten off the freeway, I had seen the sign for Donna's and had gotten a lark.

Or, rather, a craving.

These babies needed pancakes.

Nutella pancakes with crispy, salty hash browns, and a cup of decaf (and I would also have a glass of water because I was being good).

And then maybe a hot chocolate with extra whipped cream.

Because if I was having second breakfast, then I needed hot chocolate with extra whipped cream.

But first, water.

Second, order.

Third, pulling out my Kindle and diving back into my book —a romantic fantasy that was fucking incredible, the world the author had woven so well-developed and amazing and diverting that I wanted to dive in and never escape.

Oh, to be Feyre.

But I lived in the real world, with no magical, devoted, powerful men (there were powerful men and devoted men, but rarely did those worlds collide, and unfortunately none of *those* men could sprout wings or shoot lightning bolts or best beasts with nary more than their wits and a sword).

So, fantasy.

So using my vibrating friend when all my pregnancy hormones reared their needs and I got really desperate.

Sad.

But that was my life.

Because seriously, swear to Christ, it had been a long time since an actual penis had made friends with my *actual* vagina.

Plenty of tools and hands and people looking up there.

But all of them were in the business of making a baby—or babies—for Pru and Marcel, and none of them in the business of giving me an orgasm.

So...books.

So...vibrating friends.

So...shopping and chocolate-filled pancakes and my imagination.

That would be enough.

My server came out—today it was Janet—who I was on a

first-name basis with because I had come in a lot for pancakes since I'd moved down here.

One, the outlets were nearby for my favorite pastime.

Two, Donna's had delicious pancakes, Wi-Fi, and if I timed my morning drop-in just right, I could take up a booth until lunchtime and get both pancakes *and* one of their famous—at least in my book—grilled cheeses.

"Breakfast and lunch today, honey?" Janet asked, pad out and pencil already streaking across the paper.

"Just breakfast," I told her with a smile when Janet glanced up from that pad and lifted her brows. "Playing hooky from work and having a shopping extravaganza instead."

Janet smiled, wide enough that she flashed me her crooked eye tooth, and tucked her pencil back behind her ear. "Good for you," I said. "I know I've told you plenty, but you work too hard, especially with those babies cooking."

"Someone touched my belly today," I blurted.

Two someones technically.

Though my lightly calloused fingers had been welcome.

The strange woman with the boxer-like (the dog, not the profession) face had all but cornered me in the lot and asked when I was due.

It was...one of those odd wanting to commiserate about the difficulties of being a woman scenarios—or so I thought—because the woman wasn't mean and didn't give me weird vibes (other than the whole touching without permission part). But I wasn't keen to continue having discussions about my birth plan and/or breastfeeding versus formula with complete strangers.

For one, I hadn't even thought about it.

For another, I knew that I needed to scratch down researching pumping, how it worked, all the equipment I might need, and how long I should be doing it for the babies.

So, in addition to being subject to talking about boobs and

vaginas and things coming out of them, that random woman had now added more things to my To Do list.

Which wasn't cool.

"Your belly?"

I nodded.

"Did she tack on the horror of her birth story?"

Another nod. "All three of them."

Janet made a noise of disgust. "Why do people do that?"

"No clue," I whispered.

Janet shook her head, tucked her pad away. "Me neither, but I do know that Nutella pancakes fix a multitude of ailments."

"They sure do," I agreed with a smile.

"Decaf?"

I nodded for a third time. "And hot chocolate with extra whipped cream"—Janet's mouth tipped up—"and water because the doctor says I need to drink more."

"On it, sweetie," Janet said, rapping the table lightly with her knuckles. "You just settle in with your book and let me take care of you."

You just settle in with your book and let me take care of you.

That wasn't the first time Janet had said that to me, but it struck me just as hard as though it was the first time.

Because my mom used to say that.

Before...

My vision went watery, but I managed to keep my voice even as I glanced down at my hands, let that blurry vision make my skin go wavy. "Thanks, Janet," I whispered.

Another rap of her knuckles.

Then she'd left, buzzing around the dining room.

I pretended to focus on getting settled with my e-reader, fussing with getting it positioned just right, but truthfully, I was just buying time to get it together.

You just settle in with your book and let me take care of you.

The chains rattled.

Those doors bowed.

But I forced myself to focus on the page and read, drinking the water that Janet brought then alternating between the coffee and hot cocoa.

A lot of liquid, especially when Janet refilled my water, and I drank it down like the good little patient I was.

Then, of course, because it was a lot of liquid, I spent the next ten minutes wiggling on my cushion but feeling too lazy to get up and pee, and just when it got bad enough for me to consider scooting my ass out of that booth and heading to the bathroom—which was, thankfully, not too far away—Janet returned with my pancakes and hash browns, and I couldn't leave my food unattended.

Or alone.

Or lonely.

Sitting there and getting cold.

So, I got my wiggle on even as I downed my delicious pancakes and drank my refill of hot cocoa and another glass of water. I stayed on my cushion as I polished off my crispy hash browns with plenty of salt.

And stupidly, I stayed on my cushion in that booth, my plates empty, my cups empty (minus the water glass, which Janet had a spidey sense to refill), and I read until a chapter break.

Because I had to know what happened to my girl.

Because it was hot with an H. O. Double T.

I wasn't sure that was really a thing, but the scene had me so enthralled I couldn't even make fun of my own ridiculousness.

But then I finished the chapter, and I was dropped back into my reality.

Eighties explosion. Empty plates and glasses.

No mythical man racing in to save me, to pick me up in his arms, fly me away, and worship me on a mountain top—that worshipping including multiple orgasms and providing me with a whole new wardrobe.

Nope.

No magic. No flying.

Just Janet casually having placed the bill at the end of the table, leaving me to my fantasies.

Just me and those fantasies and a good book and two babies that didn't belong to me happily wiggling in my belly. And a bladder that was full and getting wiggled on and required immediate attention.

So...bill. Bathroom. Shopping.

I slipped some cash from my wallet—enough to pay for my food and leave a generous tip—chugged down the last of the water, and packed up my Kindle.

Then I slid out of the booth.

A little too fast because my head went spinny.

But I paused and sat at the edge of the booth, ignoring my bladder, breathing slow and deep and then trying again, knowing I had the ticket the second time around because there were no spots at the edges of my vision.

Then I was on my feet.

Then I was steady, and the babies were safe.

And *then*, finally, I hightailed it to the bathroom.

ELEVEN

THE GUYS HAD SOMEHOW MISSED that Beth was there, sitting a handful of booths away.

Or at least Cas and Theo had.

Smitty was still wearing his gossip face.

But I had managed to survive pancakes and conversation, and Smitty hadn't brought up the gorgeous redhead, even though I'd had to tear my gaze away from her more than a handful of times.

Drinking lots of water.

Eating heartily.

Steady and smiling at the waitress and reading her book.

Fucking beautiful. Fucking bright. Fucking...with my head.

Smitty was pushing out the door, Cas and Theo a few steps behind me, when I saw a flicker of red, and my gaze was drawn to her again.

She was sitting on the edge of the booth, brows dragged together, lips parted like she was breathing slowly.

And then she was rising slowly.

Like she was unsteady.

Cas and Theo followed Smitty out into the cool morning air, but I couldn't make my feet go. "I'm gonna use the bathroom," I muttered. "Catch you guys at the rink later."

Smitty's eyes got all gossip-centric again, but Cas and Theo just nodded, calling their goodbyes as I spun back toward the dining room...just in time to see Beth on her feet and all but racing through it for the bathrooms.

Fuck.

Fuck.

Was she sick now, too?

The door slammed shut behind me, but I didn't hear it. I was already moving after Beth, following her into the narrow hall that housed the bathrooms, waiting there because the door had already swung closed behind her.

Waiting longer, my worry prickling up my spine.

Then longer still, that worry growing to something deeper, something more all-encompassing. What if she'd fallen again?

As far as I knew, she was alone in there—no one else had gone out or come in—and if she was alone and unconscious and—

"Right," I whispered and pushed into the bathroom.

It was...empty.

Claws in my belly, raking through my insides, splitting me wide open.

"Beth," I croaked then cleared my throat. "*Beth!*"

A toilet flushed, and I realized I was a dumbass. Women's bathrooms had *stalls*, not just urinals and a single toilet crammed into the corner with a door that barely covered my ass. This was all stalls, and I hadn't looked closely enough.

Because there were feet under one.

Feet that were moving to the door, tugging it open.

Feet that belonged to Beth.

"*Raph?*" she exclaimed, smoothing down her sweater.

"Are you okay?" I asked, moving closer, gripping her shoulders. "Are you sick? Dizzy?"

"I'm fi—"

"Don't lie to me, baby. I saw you run in here and—"

She started to lift a hand, as though to push me back or to grab my hand then stopped, dropping it to her side. "I had to pee, honey," she said softly. "I drank four glasses of water, two hot chocolates, and a cup of coffee. I was too lazy to get up before I finished my pancakes, so I waited"—her mouth turned up—"until I was in an emergency situation."

Emergency—

Christ.

I shook my head.

"Now," she whispered. "Can I wash my hands?"

"You weren't just eating pancakes."

A blink.

"You were reading."

Now her cheeks went a little pink, and I began to wonder *what* she had been reading at that table.

I didn't have time to focus on that because she was frowning, spinning out of my hold, and moving to the sink. "Yeah, I was." A shrug. "I like to read."

I knew that, too.

I'd heard her and Pru and Hazel talking about books enough times during nights out to know that, to understand why my mention of reading had her blushing.

"What were you reading?" I murmured, sliding close, my voice dropping about three octaves.

I knew *that*, too.

Why it was happening, the slippery slope I was creeping toward, that I couldn't stop myself from approaching.

"I need to go," she murmured, reaching past me for a paper towel. "I have plans."

I tore off the towel for her, passed it over, watched as she dried her hands.

When she was done, I took it from her, dumped it into the trash. "What plans?"

Her eyes had been on her feet, deliberately avoiding mine, but my question had her glancing up. "Plans," she said, reaching toward me, her body moving close.

I sucked in a breath.

But she wasn't reaching for me. She was reaching beyond me again. For another paper towel, which she folded up as she moved toward the door, wrapping it around the handle and using it to tug the heavy wooden door open.

Then she waved a hand at me, directing me to precede her.

I should have opened the door. I should have held it for her.

I—

"Raph?"

A quiet question that drew my eyes to hers.

"You should probably leave the women's restroom now."

That had me jerking into motion.

I slipped out the door, moved to the side, letting her go ahead, watching her move, something relaxing in me when her gait was even, and her pace was steady.

Right.

I should probably go before I made even more of a fool of myself.

But I couldn't pry myself away from Beth's side, even as we made our way out of the restaurant, as I pushed the door open for her, as I followed her to her car.

"Raph?" she asked again as she dug in her purse for her keys.

"How'd you get your car back?"

She froze then her head jerked up. "What?"

"Your car was at CeCe's. Did Marcel or Pru get someone to bring it over?"

Teeth worrying her bottom lip, and I knew they hadn't, and suddenly I was kicking myself even harder. I'd yelled at her, made her cry, bullied her into the ER, and then left her. Then I'd broken into her house and hadn't even thought to bring her car so she'd have a way to get around.

"How?" I asked again, my fingers covering hers on the handle.

A shrug that was so casual it was almost disarming. *Almost* because I'd noticed other things about Beth besides the fact that she seemed destined to break through shields I was desperately trying to reinforce and hold in place.

Almost disarming because she was really good at getting people to look away from her.

Bright and pretty and perfectly put together.

But constantly shifting the attention from herself. Even when she was making everyone at the table laugh, usually it was at her own expense, and then, just as quickly, she was passing that attention over to someone else.

Camouflage.

But I saw her.

I couldn't ignore her, even when I was desperate to.

"I took a Lyft." Another casual shrug. "Picked up my car, planned to hit the outlets for some better clothes and save Pru the trouble of having to be my dressing room wingman." Beth's face gentled. "She offered, and I know Marcel would come with me if I asked, or Hazel, or Oliver. But"—her gaze dipped to the side, and she shrugged again—"it's my thing, not theirs."

I hated that I hadn't thought of that, hated she'd had to deal with retrieving her car after the shitty night she'd had.

Hated...

No, was *tired* of fighting so hard.

So maybe I just...needed to stop fighting.

Clearly, Beth needed someone to look after her. And no one else was around. So that someone looking after her needed to be me.

Decision made—or maybe finally accepted, considering I'd been drifting toward this outcome for months now—I asked, "Those pants the loosest ones you have?"

Her eyes widened then I watched as a mask slipped onto her face, smirk curving those red-painted lips. Disarming. Trying to put me off.

I didn't like that.

Liked it less when her tone went teasing, "What are you trying to say, Raph? That this girl is getting fat?"

I liked when she was soft with me, when she gave me a glimpse of *her* without any bullshit.

"Don't."

The way that burst out of me was visceral, and I couldn't stop it and...

It made her mask slip, thank fuck.

"Don't what?" she whispered.

"Don't do that."

"Do *what?*" she asked softly.

"You're beautiful," I said, still going on gut. "And you fucking know it."

Her lips parted, and fuck if I didn't want to kiss the lipstick off, to see the pale pink they'd been without it that morning. My lips. Only for my eyes. A shield for the rest of the world.

But not a shield for me.

Fuck. I was so totally fucked.

I pressed on anyway. "Heard you tell Pru about the clothes. Haven't seen you in much besides that sexy schoolmarm shit you normally wear."

"Sexy sch-sch—school—" She shook her head. "What?" she breathed.

"You need clothes?"

Her lips pressed flat then released. "Yes," she whispered.

I pushed her door closed, snagged the keys from her hand, and bleeped the locks. "So, we're going shopping."

"But—"

I took her elbow, led her to my car, and took advantage of her discombobulation to tuck her in the passenger's side seat, ignoring the growing feeling inside me, ignoring that it was pleased she didn't fight me, that I'd decided I was going to look after her.

A push had the door shut.

Then I was rounding the hood.

I happened to glance up, saw Smitty sitting in his car, giant shit-eating grin on his dumb face.

It said, "*Gotcha.*"

It said I was fucked.

I still got into the driver's side and turned on the engine.

And then I took Beth shopping.

TWELVE

Beth

HE HAD bags lining both arms like oversized bracelets.

And I was standing outside a store that looked really freaking awesome, teeth pressing into my bottom lip, wanting to go in, but not wanting to take advantage of the fact that I'd dragged Raph into a half-dozen stores already and had bought enough clothes to make it clear Pru didn't need to take me shopping for the next half-century, at least.

"Beth."

I didn't need those shoes, even if they were flats and had that adorable eyelet detail.

I turned away, started walking. "We should go. It's getting late."

It was early afternoon. I'd spent enough money, and even though he'd been exceptionally patient—not complaining *once* —I'd dragged him along enough places.

"Beth."

Time to go before I wore out my welcome.

Sparkly sandals with a pointed toe and heel.

Oh, Lord. Those were *beautiful.*

My feet skittered.

Straps that would crisscross over my foot, wrap around my ankle and calf.

No.

I couldn't even wear them right now, wouldn't be able to for months, not with the low blood pressure and my belly growing.

"Sugarpie."

Right. No more shoes. No more shopping.

A hand on my jaw, cupping lightly, those bags rustling and crinkling. "Beth, honey. Go try on the shoes."

"I won't be able to wear them, not for months," I whispered.

"Go try on the shoes," he repeated.

My nostrils flared, drawing in a deep breath. "I already bought enough for today."

"Can you afford the shoes?"

Considering I could go on a shopping spree every day for the rest of my days (and not at the outlets) and still not make a dent in the trust fund my mom had left me, yeah, I could afford the shoes.

"Beth?"

"Yes," I whispered.

A sparkle in his bright blue eyes. "Then, sugarpie, go try on the shoes."

I took a step toward the entrance, mostly because he let his hand fall to my lower back and nudged me forward.

Then I stopped. "You've been patient."

His big body shifted so that he was at my front, and I looked up, *way* up into his eyes. "Yeah."

"You're carrying my bags."

One brown brow lifted. "Yeah, honey."

"And you're not complaining."

A pause. "No, sugarpie."

Warmth in my belly and for a minute, the pounding at the doors in the basement quieted. Which set me spinning, had me pressing my teeth into my bottom lip, and meant that I said something that had nothing to do with our conversation and everything to do with the way this man made me feel. "I've never actually heard anyone call another person *sugarpie*."

His smile flashed, and *that* wasn't a calming warmth. It was a battering ram to my gates, a call to fling wide those doors and let the demons loose.

He'd lift his sword.

Slay them with one fell swoop.

And I was reading too many fantasy romances.

I didn't live in a world where men swept in on horses or wings that sprouted from their back, diving down, and rescuing me.

My world was...

Well, it wasn't *that*.

His fingers on my spine flexed, and years of instinct had me going still, but there wasn't a bite of pain. There weren't nails digging in, harsh words in my ear, promising pain later.

Now, it was just another nudge, another push to the door.

"Go try on the shoes, *sugarpie*."

My lips twitched. The doors rattled.

But their locks held fast.

And...I walked in through the entrance of the store.

And...I bought the sparkly sandals, the flats with the pretty detailing on top, *and* a pair of boots that I was pretty sure I was going to hell for buying.

Spike heels.

Thigh high.

Zippers along the inside.

But I'd bought them because of fire in bright blue eyes, a

muscle in his firm jaw twitching. His voice rasping, "You're getting those, or *I'm* getting them for you."

They weren't practical.

They would be sitting in my closet for months.

But that look in Raph's eyes, the huskiness of his voice. It wasn't even a second thought.

I'd bought the boots.

Raph had spent some quality time playing Jenga with my bags to get them all to fit into his trunk, and early afternoon had turned to early evening by the time that I'd finished making my way through the outlets.

I had the shoes.

I had some sweats and loose sweaters.

I had maternity jeans and tops.

I had underwear that had made fire reappear in Raph's eyes, underwear that I'd stupidly bought from a store I'd stupidly gone into. But I'd wanted to pick up some nightgowns and there had been a pretty purple lace one in the window, and then he'd leaned close and murmured, "Don't mind going into this one, sugarpie."

Sugarpie.

It was cheesy and ridiculous.

And it was the sexiest thing I'd ever heard when he leaned close and rumbled it in my ear, surrounding me with his strength and his warmth and *Raph*.

So, I'd gone in.

And...I'd gotten that violet nightgown, including a pair of pretty purple panties that went with it, along with several other matching sets of gorgeous, sensuous sleepwear.

And...I'd gotten that muscle twitch, that fire, and—

I'd decided I was going to play with it.

Stupid, huh?

But the banging in that basement, the claws gouging at the locked doors...all of that was easy to ignore when he was with me.

My stomach rumbled, and it wasn't a quiet hey-I'm-getting-hungry-so-feed-me-bitch rumble. It was a fucking *growl*, reverberating through the insides of my skeleton, echoing through the car. We'd stopped for pretzels and sandwiches a few hours before (along with the eight million bathroom stops I'd made because Raph kept reappearing with bottles of water and making me drink them).

But this was a growl, and it wouldn't be satisfied with water or pretzels or sandwiches.

It was—

My nostrils worked, the sweet scent of Donna's hitting my nose.

Oh, I wanted the apple and brie grilled cheese with fig jam. No *needed* it.

My stomach went again.

I wanted it, and wanted it now, and—

"Are you going to gnaw off your arm if I take you somewhere that's *not* Donna's?"

I blinked, so lost in my almost tasting that fig jam on my tongue that it took a minute for me to process what he was saying.

"What?" I asked, admittedly not at my finest, mostly because he was talking, and I was dreaming about fig jam and creamy brie cheese.

"How soon do you need to eat?"

Another blink. "Five minutes ago."

Something happened to his face, fire and humor mixing together with soft and gentle in his eyes, pairing with the curving of his lips, and it sent my heart skittering in a direction it had absolutely no business going.

"You good with Donna's twice in one day?"

"Will it get a fancy grilled cheese sandwich into my mouth sooner?"

A brow lifting. "A fancy grilled cheese?"

"Apples and brie and fig jam. It's an orgasm between two slices of bread." My stomach growled again at my words, and he laughed, big and loud and beautifully, and I felt like I'd felt when I'd first seen him, definitely how I'd felt the first time I'd seen him after everything had happened with his bitch of an ex—

I wanted to be the one to make him laugh.

I wanted that humor in his blue eyes to be directed at *me*. I wanted us to have inside jokes and for him to smile at me in a special way, like he had a special smile *just* for me.

I wanted him to think I was pretty and sexy and funny and smart and—

"Well, don't let it be known that I get between a woman and her orgasms."

My lungs seized.

I wanted *that*.

Heat and need and sex and orgasms. Fingers and cock and tongue. Big and hard against my soft and curved.

But...this was a lot.

This was, perhaps, too much already.

I'd get my orgasm, but it would be in the form of fruit and honey, jam and bread. It would be in the form of him carrying my bag and encouraging me to buy the shoes.

It would be in the form of a nice man looking out for me, maybe being a friend, maybe just making amends for being a bit of a jerk (and only a bit because I knew I was a lot to deal with and because I knew he'd been coping with a flurry of emotions and pain over the last year, especially with my pregnancy in his face).

But he'd move on.

They always did.

And I certainly wasn't a catch.

Pregnant, going to be getting fatter by the minute. Hormones going crazy. Low blood pressure making me a freaking nuisance. Totally high maintenance and so messed up that I was a grown woman and still using my clothes and makeup as a shield because I'd never be able to let anyone in, not really.

Despite all that, I wanted.

Him.

Me.

Together.

Swinging doors wide open and battling demons.

But...that wouldn't happen.

So, I was going to take what I could get.

Sandwiches that were almost as good as orgasms. A man holding my bags and being patient, bringing me water and looking after me because I was important to his friend.

That would be enough.

Because when I was alone, as I'd always been alone...it had always been enough.

And it would always *be* enough.

THIRTEEN

Raph

GAME NIGHT.

I'd already warmed up, done all my pregame prep, done my best to get a certain redhead out of my mind.

Shopping—which I fucking hated.

Grilled cheese sandwiches—that were really freaking good (though not as good as orgasms).

Laughter and smiles and kissable red lips—tempting, beyond tempting.

Game. Night.

Focus.

I inhaled, cleared my mind, and did just that.

As a professional hockey player, it wasn't a surprise that I had a game-day routine—a lucky pair of socks, a certain warm-up I completed, always in the same sequence (fifteen minutes on the bike, some off-ice footwork that Pru, actually, had recommended, fucking around with a roller hockey ball for a few minutes to warm up my wrists and hands, then using the time the team had on the ice to get my shots in, to get my feet under me, to make sure my equipment and blades were all in order).

Before that, I always had the same lunch, drank the same amount of water and Gatorade.

Always did the same stretches in a variety of places (post-bike, pre-ice, post-footwork).

I always got dressed in the same way.

Jock first to protect the boys, which were basically shorts with Velcro to hold up my socks and a sturdy cup shielding the business end of my junk. Then I went straight for my right shin guard, strapping it on, and over that, securing my hockey sock. Then repeating the same on my left. After that, I went to my right skate. Then left. Then my hockey pants which had pads on my thighs, hips, and a few on my ass (though not enough to protect the cheeks if I really went down hard on them).

Once that equipment was in place, it was time for hockey tape over my shin guards and socks, and not just a little of it. With shots flying my way at eighty, ninety, sometimes a hundred miles per hour, I wanted those pads to do their fucking jobs. Tape gave way to my upper body—first with elbow pads (one of the most important pieces of equipment, in my opinion, considering I usually ended up with my arms slashed to shit by the time the game was over—and was left with plenty of bruises to remind me of my elbow pads' service). I got my elbows and forearms protected and then slipped on my shoulder pads, my jersey, attaching the tie in the back of my pants that kept it in place. Then it was time for my helmet, snapping the chin strap. And finally, *finally*, I was shoving on my gloves with my mouthguard shoved in a little gap on the left one, just where the thumb pad met the curve of the side.

The last piece of equipment was my stick.

I had a whole host of them (several of each type, actually, since they broke easily). But I had a variety because each kind served a purpose—sometimes I might want to shoot more or be a bit more defensive, or sometimes the hockey gods weren't with me, and that was the first thing I swapped out.

Because clearly it was the stick.

Not me.

Anyway, it was a lot of equipment, but all of it was necessary.

I liked my body in working order, and I, most especially, liked my cock where and how it was. Not that I'd had much use for it lately.

But...those boots.

That nightgown.

Those red lips.

It had gotten a lot of use the night before. Me and my hand and jerking it till I felt raw.

"Move your ass, Gomez," Smitty boomed across the room, making me jerk something *else* (this being my head...well, the upper one, anyway).

"I'm ready, dumbass," I yelled back.

"Are you?" A brow that hinted my friend knew where my head was...and where it had been since I'd first stopped Beth from cracking *her* head on the floor of CeCe's.

I braced, readied myself for the shit-giving. Because Smitty had gossip and Smitty was a sieve and I was going to catch it... any second now.

"I expect you to get on the fucking scoresheet tonight for a change," Smitty boomed instead.

Asshole.

And a liar.

Because I had been on the scoresheet a lot that season.

I was in the top three leading scorers, had been there all year.

But I also wasn't going to cower under the force of the

Smitty Sieve, wasn't going to give an inch when I knew my teammate would take a mile. Which was why I launched my glove at Smitty, grinning when I beaned him right in the head.

Smitty, who wasn't expecting it and had turned away, squealed like a little bitch.

The room exploded with laughter.

"Motherfucker!" Smitty boomed, reaching for the glove.

Cas saved me, bending and scooping up the glove before Smitty could reach it, tossing it—*nicely*—back to me.

"Thanks, buddy," I called.

"No, thank *you*," Cas called back. "Someone's gotta shut him up."

Smitty glared.

The guys busted up again.

Then Smitty smirked, shook his head. "Yeah," he said. "You want to shut me up, don't you?"

Okay, so perhaps taunting the beast hadn't been a good idea, even *if* I was accepting that my interest in Beth would be a locker room topic. Smitty's question was ominous, and it sent a curl of fear coiling through my belly.

Fuck.

I got where this was going, and I knew it was going to happen. But still, I really didn't want to go there, didn't want the gossip train barreling down on me.

It would come.

But...fuck, I needed more time to come to terms with whatever the fuck was going on in my head.

Not that I was going to let Smitty know he had me over a barrel.

Not that I was going to give Smitty a chance to reveal what he'd seen over pancakes or in that parking lot.

I opened my mouth—

"Game time, bitches!" Theo yelled, poking his head in the door.

Always first on the ice, that one.

The guys began hopping up, moving to the door, creating the usual pregame chaos and noise, thankfully cutting Smitty off before I could demand an answer to that ominous question or say anything further.

Saved by Theo.

Yeah, I was going to buy my bud a beer the next time we were out.

Grinning, I picked up the stick I always used at the beginning of the first period, stood, and rolled my shoulders, making certain all my equipment felt right. Then I took advantage of everyone heading out, the distraction of the game starting to avoid Smitty, move into the hall, and line up with the other guys. We all did the usual manly B.S., smacking each other with our sticks, punching each other in the shoulders, unleashing plenty of pointless shit-talk.

Getting ready to fucking *go*.

Like I said, the usual.

Eventually, we got the high sign and started hustling down the hallway and onto the ice, emerging through the smoke and flashing lights, skating a couple of laps, getting that final bit of warm-up beneath us as the game song played loudly and the crowd screamed encouragements.

After a few minutes, we moved to the bench, the bright lights overhead flicking on, illuminating the arena, and someone sang the National Anthem.

Not *my* anthem, since I was Canadian, but an anthem I'd heard enough over the years to know every word.

I couldn't say it had me feeling particularly patriotic.

It was, however, another step in the building blocks of me getting ready to play some fucking *hockey*.

A breath, my shoulders bouncing, head shifting side to side. Skates wiggling beneath me, pulse picking up. It didn't matter how many times I played in this arena, how many professional games I had under my belt, always—*always*—there were nerves, there was excitement.

It was like I was lacing up my skates for the first time again, hopping out onto the ice for my first game ever.

The one thing in my life that had never disappointed me.

The anthem wrapped up. My pulse sped. Hands twitched.

Fucking game time.

Marcel smacked his stick across my shin guards. "Let's fucking go, yeah?"

We were playing the Sierra, the newest team in the league, and contrary to most expansion teams, this northern California squad was a tough match-up. The Breakers only had two games against them during the entire season—once on home ice and once away—and the match we'd had up at the Sierra's home rink in Tahoe a few months back hadn't gone well.

Part was we weren't used to playing at altitude.

Part was we weren't used to playing at that new rink.

Part was that the Sierra's management had put together a solid team who had surprised us and had solidly beat us.

Total bullshit.

We prided ourselves on our preparation, and we hadn't been ready. On the flip side, getting our asses kicked meant that I was ready to go that night. This was our home ice. Our fans. Our chance to prove that we weren't just a sad-ass team that was easily beat. We were a fucking *contender* who'd won two Cups in recent years, and we were going to win another one.

Unfortunately, the Sierra were a contender, too.

So, this game was going to be *intense*.

Redemption for the team. Keeping their feet on the gas for

the Sierra. And close enough to the playoffs that both teams wanted the two points badly enough to battle for them.

It began right at puck drop—which I won, damn right—and immediately my hands stung because I got slashed to shit for my trouble. But I ignored the burn, ignored the pain, and broke free of the lockup, shoving against the Sierra's captain, Lake Jordan. A pretty son of a bitch who had a wicked wrist shot and a penchant for making players pay if they lost a face-off.

Free of the hold, I charged into the opposing zone, Marcel carrying the puck over the blue line, trying to connect with Theo, who was playing on the other side.

I wasn't a natural center or hadn't been until Marcel had hurt his wrist earlier in the season and had missed two games.

I'd stepped into the role, had found a newfound knack for face-offs, and Marcel had slipped back into playing left wing again, and since Theo had done some time as a center himself— in fact, the team was stacked pretty effectively in that position —the three of us had found that we had even *more* good juju playing together. We knew where each other would be, we could all cover for any defensive holes that might appear, and since we'd all done time as centers, we could be flexible and get creative.

It was fucking *fun* playing together.

And our line's stats showed it.

Tonight, we weren't lucky enough to get a goal on the first shift of the game, but we got some solid pressure, a shot that went wide, and then a face-off in the zone when it deflected off a stick and hit the netting.

I wanted to stay on the ice.

I wanted to play longer.

A face-off in the o-zone? Pressure already on a team that had gotten the better of us before?

Fuck yeah, I wanted to stay.

But...this was a team sport, and we were successful because we worked together. So, I paused at that whistle, and I moved to the bench, letting Walker's line hit the ice.

Still sitting and now watching impatiently as Jackson led *his* line out for a shift.

Then even more impatiently as Flynn—the former first line center who was battling back from a knee injury—took his boys, two rookies, out for a turn about the rink.

Flynn peeled off the rush, headed for the bench.

And, fucking *finally*, it was my turn to get at it again.

The world shrank down to the rink, to the ice, my teammates, the puck.

It was fucking glorious.

It was everything I'd ever wanted.

I moved to take the face-off. Lost it. Got the puck back, started hauling ass up the rink.

And as I skated, as I carried the puck up and managed to hand it off to Theo—who buried it in the back of the net—I could almost convince myself that it was *all* I'd ever wanted.

FOURTEEN

Beth

I WAS SITTING with Hazel and Oliver, along with a plethora of girls from the team he helped coach, watching the Breakers play.

The girls were awesome, and somehow, I'd gotten seated next to one named Hannah, who was all fire and excitement and intensity.

Her gaze had been locked on the ice during every second of play.

But before the game had started and during any stoppage, including the longer pauses in the match that coincided with commercial breaks from the television feed, she'd been peppering me with questions.

Surprisingly, about makeup and clothes.

Apparently, Hazel had made me out to be the knowledge-keeper of all things girlie.

And apparently, tough as nails, intensely watching, very talented (according to Oliver) hockey player Hannah wanted a breakdown of all things that involved smoky eyes and fake lashes and matching outfits.

She was too little for it all.

But...she wasn't.

I remembered the excitement of makeup and pretty clothes and shoes and earrings and *accessories*. I remembered how fun it was playing around with them, how exciting it was to learn what I liked and to experiment and—

Then it had become a chore.

And now...I was realizing that sometime in the last decade it had become less of a chore and more fun.

Still a mask.

Still something I had to get perfect.

But talking to Hannah I suddenly had a hankering to try a new shade of eyeliner. "Tell you what," I said as the guys lined up for the face-off (and I didn't miss that one of those guys was Raph).

"What?" Hannah asked when I got a little sidetracked, lost for a moment in the fact that it wasn't fair Raph looked sexy in a helmet.

He should look dumb.

Not even more gorgeous.

"What?" Hannah asked again, a bit more impatient.

I pulled it together. "If your grown-ups say it's okay, you and your teammates can come over. I'll make pizzas and cookies, and I'll show you how to do your makeup and hair."

"Really?" No impatience. Just excitement.

"Really," I said. "Think of it as team bonding."

"That. Is. *Awesome!*" Hannah yelled, turning her attention back to the ice.

Just as the puck dropped.

Raph didn't get control of that one. It flew back between the Sierra player's feet and skidded toward his defenseman. But

Raph was moving, barreling toward that puck, on a mission, and on a mission that succeeded when he snagged it and managed to get it over to Theo, who carried it down into the zone and scored, burying it decisively behind the goalie's shoulder.

The crowd erupted.

I felt it in my belly, felt the babies roll and move.

"This is the best day *ever!*" Hannah yelled, fist-pumping and then doing a little dance that I found myself on my feet joining in with.

It was too cute *not* to.

"Woo!" I cheered, fist-bumping Hannah as we finished our little jig.

A flash of blue.

My eyes drawn to the glass.

Raph was on the other side.

And the look on his face...it had every bit of air inside me going solid.

His lips moved, but I couldn't read them.

Not until he smiled, mischief in his blue eyes.

Sugarpie.

He was calling me sugarpie and pressing his hand onto the glass, and I was lifting mine to line it up to his like this was a bad drama film, and he was heading off for war or something.

In front of twenty thousand people.

Then he was gone, and my cheeks were hot—though, thank fuck, I had my makeup on so no one would be able to see I was blushing. No one being Hannah and her teammates. No one being Hazel and Oliver, whose faces I caught a glimpse of when my gaze darted to the side—Hazel, considering with no little amount of caution tossed in; Oliver, pure shit-eating amusement. No one being whoever of the twenty thousand people in the sold-out arena happened to be looking up at the jumbotron and saw me reenacting my wartime dramatic film with Raph.

"Fuck," I whispered under my breath, thankful it was loud enough in the arena for the girls not to hear me.

Thankful that the game moved right along, my and Raph's interaction a short blip in the action.

Because the Sierra came right back, putting a ton of pressure on the Breakers and keeping them chasing in their own zone for several breath-stealing minutes.

Lots of shots.

Lots of near misses.

Lots of oohs and ahhhs from the crowd.

Then Cas got the puck, and the big, lanky defenseman glanced up the ice...and I held my breath, finally understanding a bit of the game when I saw the lane to the net—I *actually* saw it, saw the space, the path he could take, the opening around the players.

He'd seen it, too, and a lot faster than me, no surprise.

He was already moving, charging up the ice, closing in on the Sierra goalie.

A shot...

The crowd groaned.

But that shot was hard and low and the puck bounced off his pads...right to Raph.

He swung, his stick flicking out, and this time the crowd erupted.

Because the puck flew into the goal.

Hannah and I were on our feet again, the babies rolling, my butt jiggling, my voice ringing out with the rest of the Breakers fans in the arena.

Raph was mobbed by his teammates, and they all started skating to the bench, but I didn't miss him turning to look at me, his eyes flaring, mouth tipping up at one end before his lips moved, and this time I almost heard his voice rasping in my ear. "For you, sugarpie."

So fucking ridiculous.

So fucking lame.

Such a fucking *line*.

But…it wasn't. I'd known him long enough to know that was for *me*.

A wink. That mouth turning up again, this time on both sides.

And then he was back on the bench.

And then Hazel was leaning close, *her* mouth tipped up. "I think we need to talk."

Nope. No talking. I had the all-encompassing urge to run up the stairs and out of this arena, to keep on running back to New York, maybe up to Canada to some small farm town where the copious winter storms would keep everyone at bay.

But I couldn't run.

I was cooking two babies for Pru and Marcel.

I was building a life here for myself.

I was locking those demons down *forever* so that I could have a happy life, a peaceful life. Auntie to my friends' kids, soaking up all of their joy so that I didn't risk rattling the demons who were hanging out in the dungeon, didn't risk setting them free. I would be the best bridesmaid-slash-co-maid-of-honor I could be. The best travel buddy. The best babysitter. I would always bring a pie or hosting a pizza and makeup party or cook dinner or…I would make a small space for myself in my friends' lives.

I would survive on that.

But letting anyone in deeper?

I couldn't do that.

Couldn't risk it.

Not even if the message from all the romance novels I read

was to be open, to be vulnerable, to hand over those demons so my *man* could slay them.

My hero didn't have wings.

My hero didn't carry a sword.

My hero didn't have a morally gray conscience that would have him burn down the world for *me*.

My hero didn't exist.

"I don't think you two need to talk," Oliver quipped, causing me to blink, to jerk out of my own head. He winked at me, directed his comment at his wife. "I think all Beth needs is a jersey with the number eighty-two on it."

Raph's number.

Raph's jersey.

"I guess don't need to keep worrying about finding an excuse to pull him in for a talk anymore," Hazel said back, smile growing as she squeezed my hand. "I know my girl will take good care of him."

Because that's what I did.

I stepped in.

I made things right.

But then I stepped right back out, slipping into the background, letting the happiness of fixing and helping and making right fuel me.

That was what I did for my charities.

That was what I was doing for Pru and Marcel.

That was what I would do with babysitting and friends' vacations and Cheese Night Extravaganza. I fixed, but my castle gates stayed firmly closed...or at least the doors to the basement were securely locked (in the case of Pru and Hazel since they were closer to me than anyone else and actually had made it inside the castle's first floor).

But even as I thought that, about all the security methods in place, my stomach churned and worry bubbled through my veins.

Because Raph didn't strike me as the type of man who would be satisfied to be locked outside of heavy castle gates or be barred from an entire floor.

He didn't have wings.

He couldn't fly.

His conscience wasn't gray, and he wouldn't burn down the world.

But he had skates.

So maybe he could *fly* that way.

Fly right across the ice, sail through the walls.

And reduce my castle to rubble.

FIFTEEN

Raph

"YOU KNOW YOU FUCKED UP, RIGHT?" Smitty muttered as he dropped onto the bench in the locker room next to me.

"How? Saving your ass in our zone?" I asked. "Or by taking that shot off my foot when Marty couldn't get across the crease to make that save?"

Because the last still fucking hurt.

Would be throbbing for days.

My snark got me a punch to the shoulder—hard, though not hard enough to really hurt.

Just hard enough for Smitty to remind me of his strength.

It wasn't nearly as hard as that puck I'd taken to my foot, and I was just thanking the hockey gods I'd begun wearing thick plastic coverings on my skates. I wore them every game after I'd broken a bone in my foot a few seasons before. Without them, that block tonight would have definitely cracked another bone, and it had hurt enough that I wasn't looking forward to taking my skate off.

Samantha, our head trainer, would get me right, I knew.

But that didn't mean I wouldn't be sporting a monster bruise and sore ass foot for a few too many days.

"With Beth."

I blinked, glanced up from my skates, and saw the knowledge in Smitty's eyes.

Fuck.

Yeah. *That.*

I knew I fucked up with showing *that,* not only to my teammates, but to the arena full of Breakers fans.

But I'd seen her there with Oliver and Hazel, with Hannah and her teammates doing a fucking dance that was somehow both sexy and adorable—enough of the first that my dick had twitched in my cup (ouch) and plenty of the second that I'd seen more than one set of male eyes on her (even with that baby belly).

I'd caught a glimpse of her dancing with that little girl, her belly rounded, and...

I'd wanted.

No.

I'd wanted her for a long time, but I'd ignored it because of Monica, because of the complication of dating someone who was close with my friends. I'd ignored it, even as that wanting grew.

But I was at a breaking point.

Or maybe that had been at CeCe's a few days ago.

Seeing her fall, witnessing the tears, the shadows, the way she tucked them all away and reassured her friend when it was clear that she was far from that after her nightmare that had woken her not knowing where or when she was. Then she'd gone shopping for clothes she needed because she was doing something big for those friends and their babies needed it, not blinking when they weren't her usual style, wearing them as she danced with a little girl, and smiling at me through the glass like I was a lunatic when I called her sugarpie.

I couldn't ignore Beth.

Not anymore.

Not the way she looked through the window of the shoe store, teeth pressing into that bottom lip, like she was worried I was going to run out of patience or she was going to use up my good will, even though I was the one who'd all but bullied myself into the trip.

I fucking hated shopping.

But…I didn't mind going with Beth.

Hell, I'd gotten off on thinking about her wearing those boots she'd bought, the panties and nightgown.

I didn't mind schlepping her shit because I knew she was okay, knew she was eating and drinking enough, knew that she was *with me.*

Trouble.

I was in so much fucking trouble.

And I didn't mind that either.

"Hey, dopey." Smitty punched me again, and I realized a bunch of the guys were moving out of the main locker room, having tossed their gear in the various bins and cubbies, their jerseys in another. I was still fully dressed, only having dropped my stick in the rack outside the door. "Pull it together before Beth sees you being a dumbass on camera."

Unfortunately, Smitty was right.

I'd had a good game, had already been given the high sign that I was going to have a few interviews. At least one of those would probably be on camera, so if I didn't want to look dopey sitting there in my full gear, including my helmet, I should probably get moving.

So I did.

First my helmet then slipping off my jersey, shoulder pads and ignoring Smitty when he mouthed, "Beth." A toss had the jersey in the bin, a twist had my pads hung up, my helmet on the shelf, and I had just enough time to plunk a hat on my sweaty-ass hair before the press came in.

Most of the questions were the same typical shit—how'd it felt to get a win, why we got it this time and not before, what was the outlook for the rest of the season.

But there was a new woman asking questions that were smarter and a hell of a lot more fun to answer than the typical stuff.

From what I knew of Eva Moreno, she was a blogger and podcaster, and had recently been picked up to do some commentating for a local sports show.

I could also see that she was gorgeous and smart...

And her eyes kept drifting toward Theo as I talked.

Maybe I should be offended, considering Theo seemed to be deliberately avoiding any and all eye contact with the pretty blond reporter, but instead, my spidey senses were prickling.

Hmm.

Watching that showdown was definitely more fun than being on the receiving end of Smitty's attention about Beth.

Plus, Theo needed a good woman.

"Right," Eva said, hitting the button to stop the recording app and tucking her cell away. "Thanks for your time."

I nodded. "Of course." Then couldn't resist adding, "Though Theo might have something more to say about it."

A flash in her coffee-colored eyes, maybe annoyance, maybe trepidation, but she didn't back off like I half expected. Instead, her chin came up, and I watched her shoulders straighten as she pulled out her cell again. Then she marched over to Theo.

Whose eyes flared with something that had me knowing a showdown between him and Eva definitely would be fun to watch.

Yeah, so much more fun being on this end.

And yeah, just call me Smitty for all my nosiness and matchmaking tendencies.

Grinning, I moved in through the door and down the hall to the private locker room, where the guys could cool down, shower, and dress without the risk of cameras catching anything...or in actuality, without the cameras catching Smitty's naked ass strutting through the room "air-drying" because he couldn't be bothered with a towel.

Like right then.

Because seriously, I entered the space and immediately saw Smitty.

Naked and coming out of the shower.

Sigh.

"Christ," I muttered, moving to grab a towel, and tossing it at him.

Smitty caught it...and wiped his face, leaving ass and junk on full display.

I reached for my shirt, tugging it up and over my head. "Christ."

"You said that already." Beard and hair toweled off, Smitty tossed the towel in the rolling cart before moving over to his station.

Yeah, I had.

And I'd probably say it a million more times when dealing with Smitty over the years.

Knowing there wasn't anything else to be done about it, I just shook my head and hit the showers himself.

But when I came out, I did it with a towel around my waist.

Unfortunately, when I came out, it wasn't to an empty room.

Nope.

Smitty was sitting right next to my cubby.

Barely holding back a groan but knowing there was nothing to be done about it, I hit the bench and started getting dressed. Underwear, socks, pants, shirt. I'd come in a suit, but I couldn't stand collared shirts post game. The pants were fine because they were tailored to me. The shirt was, too, but hell, I fucking hated how tight they always felt around my neck.

So, I waited until last to button that up.

And then I skipped my fair share of buttons so I could fucking *breathe*.

Smitty, meanwhile, was in sweats and a tee, his ugly ass suit on a hanger and ready to be carried home. The pattern hurt my eyes, but Smitty never seemed to run out of even uglier and more *plaidy* suits.

"Beth," Smitty said.

Right.

My teammate was a dog with a bone, and I knew I had two choices—lie about my interest, or just admit to it, take the interference, and then mobilize the full force of the Breakers and all their nosy meddling.

The lie was on the tip of my tongue.

What came out instead was, "Yeah."

And then instead of Smitty grinning and slapping me on the back, congratulations booming through the room, as I had expected, my friend and teammate's face went serious and he said, "Fuck, man, are you sure?"

SIXTEEN

Beth

I WAS ON THE COUCH, even though I hadn't had any more episodes of dizziness, when I heard the bolt scrape in the lock.

It wasn't fear that slid through me at that sound.

It was...anticipation.

I'd known he was going to come, had seen it in his eyes, knew it in my gut.

Just like I knew I was going to take care of him, to try my best to keep him outside the castle gates. And worst case, to get him sorted, I would consider letting him into the first floor. Of course, I'd make doubly sure that the basement was extra, super-duper barricaded, just in case.

Because I didn't like to think about what was down there.

And I was never, *ever* going to tell anyone about it.

The way the police had looked at me, how my *family* had looked at me, the whispered words and sharp glances...no.

Just...*no*.

The physical door swung open at the same time I threw my mental door, locking that shit down.

Raph crept in.

I didn't need the lights on to know it was him. I'd watched him enough to have memorized his body, his gait. He closed the door almost silently behind him and then moved into the entryway, body turning and freezing when he saw I was sitting up on the couch.

Wearing the thigh-high boots and a jersey with his name and number on it...

I'd hit the pro shop during intermission.

I'd picked up the jersey after the game.

Was I sliding down a stupid slippery slope that was going to end up with my heart broken and Raph hopefully understanding that not all women were like Monica? Yup. Was I being a presumptuous mofo who thought that I could fix a good man? Also, yup. But I was good at caring for people, for giving them the pieces.

And like I'd said, Raph was a good person.

I wanted to give him the pieces to make a good life.

I dropped my feet to the floor, pushed up to standing.

"Beth."

It was a rasp, dragging over my skin like it was his tongue making patterns, raising goose bumps.

"Oliver said I needed your jersey."

I spun slowly, showing him my back, and felt the air in the room grow still. But it wasn't cold. It was scorching hot, leaving my skin feeling charred, as though if I ran my fingers over the surface, it would all turn to ash.

He took one step toward me. Stopped.

"Why?" he croaked.

It was easy to lock everything up and just be in the moment when he sounded like that, when I was watching every line of his body being held in taut control. Except his hands. His hands were shaking.

Until he clenched them in fists at his sides.

"Why?" I asked, playfulness coursing through me.

He was a big bad hockey player, and I could see that his control was splintering, that he was on the edge and holding himself back...and I wanted to tease him.

"Yeah. Why?"

Hoarse words.

Another step.

More halting, his body practically vibrating now.

Moisture between my legs, need coiling through my belly, reminding me I hadn't had a man in a long time, hadn't had anyone down there who wasn't a doctor trying to put these babies in my belly.

I wanted Raph.

I wanted to make him smile and laugh and to brighten his day.

I wanted to make him lose control.

I wanted just a little more of him being soft, his care, just a little bit more of him bringing me water and looking at me with gentle eyes and making me toast.

Until he realized what I was, where he would never get.

Until he understood that I was too much trouble.

Until he gave up and left.

Until—

"Beth."

My name was sharp, and I blinked, threw the heavy log that would secure the gates, and shut everything down except for this moment, this man, the heat of his gaze, the way his body and hands shaking had desire slinking through me.

"Sugarpie," I said understanding what he wanted, that he needed to know why I was doing this, wanting the explanation.

"And water bottles and fancy grilled cheese and toast with strawberry jelly. And"—my voice dropped—"you seem to finally want me, too."

Between one blink and the next, he was in front of me, his body close enough for me to feel the heat of his.

"I've always wanted you."

A sharp inhale, the babies' movements picking up speed. "What?" I breathed on the exhale.

His eyes blazed. "I saw those red lips and wanted them wrapped around my cock."

My heart had been beating fast, and I hadn't realized *quite* how quickly until it increased its pace with those words, thudding against my rib cage, making it so my breaths were coming in rapid inhales and exhales.

"I saw that ass, those breasts, that face. Heard your laugh, watched you toss your hair and give Oliver and Marcel and Smitty—and even me—shit and I knew that you'd fucking ruin me, baby."

I couldn't form words.

Could just suck in another breath.

"I *wanted* that ruin," he whispered. "But then Monica came up pregnant"—a cruel smile—"or lied about it, and I put you out of my mind." A beat, his eyes going soft. "I'm not a cheater."

No. I knew him well enough to understand how important loyalty was.

"And anyway, you belonged to Pru and Hazel," he went on. "If it went wrong, then shit at work would get complicated. And I like my work. Hockey is the one thing that has always made sense in my life." A shake of his head. "I don't put that at risk, not ever."

"I'm not like that," I whispered back. "I wouldn't do anything to—"

Fingers on my bottom lip, dragging lightly across. "I know." A breath. "Which is why this day has been coming from the moment I met you."

Now *my* hands were shaking.

With need.

Because *that* was enough. His words *were enough.*

He'd wanted me then. He wanted me now.

He knew I wasn't the kind of woman who would ever mess up his work.

And...he was here, his eyes a mix of hot and soft and...I, God, I wouldn't ever be strong enough to turn that down.

So, I spun, taking a step away from him. Far enough that he could see what was on the back of the jersey—his name, his number. Far enough away that he could see that the jersey with his name and number was obscenely short, just teasing the backs of my thighs. And when I bent away from him, hitched my ass back as I angled at the waist, ensuring that the hem lifted a bit higher, I knew he saw what I'd intended—my lacy, royal blue panties that revealed more than they covered— because he groaned.

"Fuck, Beth."

There was nothing better than when a man growled a woman's name like that.

It was a tongue and fingers between my thighs, a cock plunging deep. It was a declaration wrapped in desire and...it was *mine.*

My name.

My man wanting *me.*

"I don't know what's better," he growled, wrapping his hand around my arm and spinning me to face him. "Those panties, the boots, or the jersey."

"Well, which one do you want to take off first?" I asked, tapping a finger to my lips.

A flash of white teeth, his blue eyes ablaze. "All of it."

I laughed, shook my head. "Then I don't know which is better either."

"Beth?"

My laughter cut off at the seriousness of his tone. "Yeah?"

"You sure?"

"That I want to fuck you?" I asked, lightly, because that should be fucking obvious by the way I was dressed, how I'd thrown myself at him time and again. But when I saw what was in his expression, how it was minus the flash of white teeth, the amusement in his eyes, I had my tone going just as serious as his had been. "Or am I sure that I want to open this can of worms?"

He didn't reply to the quiet question.

But he didn't have to.

Because I knew what was in his head.

Because I was going to make this better.

"I'm not Monica," I whispered, watching his face tighten. "And I wouldn't fuck you over. Not because you don't deserve it—because obviously you don't. *No one* deserves to be treated like that." His jaw flexed, and I smoothed my hand over the hard lines. "But I wouldn't do that to you specifically because I think you're sexy and kind, and I like how you care about your friends, how you're always there to step in for them and take their backs. I wouldn't do that because you're good at your job, because you call me sugarpie, even though that's cheesy as fuck."

That jaw relaxed, amusement finally entered his eyes. "You like it."

I did.

A lot.

Probably too much, all things considered.

But that amusement was perfect.

It was sexy. It gave me the courage to keep moving forward.

"And," I said softly. "I wouldn't do that because you're *you.*"

The doors buckled...held.

And then I wasn't thinking about doors at all.

Because Raph was stepping close, his body pressing to mine. Because he was reaching down, hands cupping my ass over the lace of my panties.

Warm, rough palms.

Big strong body.

Lifting me...then turning and carrying me up the stairs.

"Raph?" I asked when we were halfway up.

"Yeah, honey?"

"I—" I paused, nibbled on my bottom lip. "I—" A shake of my head.

"What, baby?"

Honey. Baby.

Only my mom and Pru and Hazel had given me that.

I'd given it. I'd asked for it from the few men I'd dated.

But I'd never been given it freely, and that—

Wasn't what I should be focused on at that moment. This was about what I could do for a good man who was sexy and made my body sing...and he hadn't even kissed me yet.

Oh, God.

Let him be a good kisser.

Pretty puh-lease.

"Beth?"

Right. I was supposed to be talking. "I haven't done this in a while," I whispered. "And it goes without saying"—I waved my hand in the direction of my belly—"I haven't done it with all this."

He didn't reply, so I kept blabbering.

"So, I don't know how I feel or what will feel good or what spots—"

He shifted, bringing his hand and cupping my jaw. "So, we'll figure it out."

"I—"

"It's been more than a year for me," he said, straight out, shocking the shit out of me. A *year?* This man, and all his gorgeousness, both inside and out, hadn't been with a woman for a *year?* "So, if anyone should be worried, it's me and the fact that I might get the tip of my dick in you and come like a sixteen-year-old boy who's just getting his first foray into pussy."

"I—" A sharp shake of my head then I could only whisper, "A year, honey?"

No sign of embarrassment. No pink on his cheeks, and his eyes didn't slide away from mine, just held fast and I saw the blip of amusement pass through those pretty blue irises. "My forearm has gotten quite the workout, so when I tell you I'll figure it out, I mean *we'll* figure it out, sugarpie. I'll probably blow like the Fourth of July finally having you after wanting you for so long, but I promise"—those blue irises went intent, and I meant *intent*—"I'll get you off first."

Okay, that was fucking hot.

It probably shouldn't have been, considering he was saying he was going to be a quick trigger. But...it was for me. He wanted *me*. He'd wanted me for a while. And he didn't just let anyone get in there, to get close, to have *this,* and he wanted *me*.

Me.

My pulse sped, hope blossoming heady and wide, mixing with him giving it to me straight, with honesty that might not be flowery and poetic, but was the truth, and that meant more than any freaking sonnet. And add in honey and baby and *we'll,* and this man was very close to giving me something important and big and altering.

But I couldn't focus on that. On the *worry* of what that

might bring, what it might do to me. On how much that made me yearn for all those unknowns.

Because he dropped his head, spoke against my lips, asking, "Okay?"

I sensed that he needed me to be okay with that, even though the worry was marching through the basement in my mind, gleefully knocking on doors, taunting the monsters.

This wasn't what I'd signed up for.

Him giving. Me receiving, opening myself up to...

But his mouth was against mine, his blue eyes were wide and beautiful and gentle, so I stopped thinking about demons and doors and just whispered, loving the way the word felt with his lips pressed to mine, "Okay."

"Okay," he repeated, lips twitching...and then he was moving again.

And *then* he was kissing me.

And it was good—so *fucking* good.

So good I knew he was going to be good at a *lot* of things.

Thank the hockey gods.

SEVENTEEN

Raph

HER LIPS WERE SOFTER than I'd expected, and she tasted sweet.

Like apples or cherries.

No. Like strawberries.

That thought had my lips moving into a smile against hers... and in the next instant my smile was fading because her tongue slipped out and brushed lightly against the seam of my mouth.

My cock was already hard.

That tentative touch of her tongue had it aching.

But it *didn't* have me freezing.

Nope. It had me knowing that I needed to get into her bed before I fucked her right there on the top of the stairs. Normally, I wouldn't have bothered carrying her up at all, not when I could have just as easily dropped her onto the couch, fucked her hard and furious right then and there.

But...it was Beth.

And I needed plenty of space for her.

And I needed plenty of space to care for her.

She wasn't a quick fuck. She was—God help me for the slippery, frightening slope I'd just dove headfirst down—*more.*

I'd known it when she passed out at CeCe's.

I'd known it with the tears in my car.

I'd known it with the nightmare.

I'd known it with how she banked her fears and talked Pru down.

I'd known it over pancakes, over pretzels, over fancy grilled cheeses.

Hell, if I was looking deep and getting my head on straight, I'd known it from the first glimpse of those red lips, those curves, that velvet rasp of her laughter.

Fucking around. I'd been fucking around in my own misery, and that shit wasn't going to happen again.

No fucking way.

So, our first time wasn't going to be with her or me crammed into the cushions or spent bending her over the arm of the couch—though both of those quickly etched themselves on my mental list of things I wanted to do to and with her, joining in with my plans to fuck her on that little table in her entryway, on her kitchen island, on the hood of my car.

In the shower. Yeah, I also definitely had to have her in the shower.

But...bed.

That's where I wanted her for the first time.

All spread out with plenty of light overhead so I could see every luscious inch of her.

So I moved, carrying her up the remaining stairs, looking through open doors until I found her bedroom, flicking on the lights and bringing us both across the space in efficient quick steps.

Then she was on her back on the mattress.

And then I was on top of her, my weight braced on my hands.

Hell fucking yeah.

"Raph?" she asked tentatively, and I wondered if it was more worry because of the pregnancy, because of the changes in her body, because she wasn't sure what would or wouldn't feel good in this moment.

So even as I pressed my nose to her throat, inhaled that soft fruity, floral scent, I made a vow that if the tentative came from that, then I was going to make it my fucking *job* to show her how beautiful she was, how much I wanted her, babies in her belly or not. "Yeah, sugarpie?"

A pause that had me lifting my head, staring into her face as she warred with something.

But just as quickly as I'd noticed it, the battle ended.

"Will you kiss me again?" she asked softly.

My lips tipped up. "Yeah, honey."

Then I sat back.

Her brows lifted, dragged together. "Um, Raph?"

Fuck, I liked the sound of my name on her lips. My feet hit the floor and I kicked off my shoes. "Yeah?"

"I thought you were gonna kiss me." Quiet words that had my dick twitching.

I reached for the button of my slacks, flicked it open, shoved them down and stepped out of them. "I am."

"Just saying"—her voice was tinged with confusion—"that's not you kissing me."

"No," I agreed, retrieving my wallet from my slacks, tossing it on the nightstand before working on the buttons of my shirt.

Her gaze caught on my chest as I peeled the fabric open.

Yeah, I liked that.

Probably too fucking much, considering I was a year out

from being in a woman and just the feel of her eyes on my body brought me dangerously close to the edge of my control.

Probably too fucking much, considering I was nearly willing to go full striptease on her if it meant those hot blue eyes stayed glued to my body.

But I had a mind to kiss her.

I had a mind to kiss her somewhere *very* specific.

So I dropped the shirt to the floor, moved back to the bed, and instead of crawling up next to her and slanting my mouth over hers, I reached for the tag of the zipper that ran the entire inside of her boot and began sliding it down, revealing her creamy skin inch by inch.

"Raph?"

"Hmm?" I'd reached her ankle and shifted, pressing my mouth to the opening I'd created at the top, parting the leather and dragging my tongue down her leg, nibbling along the flesh of her thigh, dipping down behind her knee, finding a sensitive spot there that had her squirming. Then continuing to part that fabric, kissing along her calf, that delicate bone at her ankle, slipping the boot from her foot.

A kiss to the top of her foot, to each of the toes polished in a bright red color that matched that red lipstick of hers that drove me crazy.

Lipstick I was going to finish kissing off her in short order.

But first—

I let the boot drop, repeated my trek with my mouth. The zipper on her other boot slowly inching down, lips and mouth and tongue moving on her skin.

Teeth on her sensitive flesh.

The soft hiss of her breath. Her hips rocking on the mattress, seeking purchase as I moved, tugging the boot free, massaging her foot for a few moments.

The jersey had rucked up, exposing those panties, the curve of her belly.

And for once, it wasn't a source of pain and grief.

It was beautiful, her body creating something that had been made out of love—love of a father and mother, love of a friend—her body protecting and housing and growing.

Because I was seeing that she was a woman who cared and gave and sacrificed herself.

Because I was seeing *that*, seeing that she very rarely took, and getting her to do so was a battle because it was so foreign to her.

Because I was seeing that I was going to have to be the man to give that to her.

Starting now.

Starting with this moment.

I wrapped my fingers around her ankles, tugged, drawing her ass toward the side of the mattress, positioning her so I could kiss her exactly where I was so desperate to.

"Raph," she gasped, but I had her right where I wanted, right where we both needed, and that was on the edge of the bed, her pussy mere centimeters from my mouth. Close enough that I could see the lace was soaked. Close enough I could smell the tangy, fruity scent of her. Close enough that I could reach for the waistband of her panties and yank them down her legs, let them fall free off her ankles, drop to the floor. "Honey," she began, hands pushing lightly at my shoulders. "I've been out all day and haven't washed up—"

I dragged my tongue through her folds. "Tastes fucking good to me, sugarpie."

She shivered. "Okay." It was a whisper, a heated one, so I dragged my tongue through her labia again, tasting her, getting her used to my touch, watching her face and body to find the spots that had her squirming, trying not to get distracted by the round globes of her breasts peeking out from where the jersey was bunched up.

Already, my cock was aching.

Already, my hands were shaking.

Already, I wanted to cover her with my body, plunge deep over and over again and let blissful oblivion overtake me.

But I didn't move from my knees at the edge of the bed. I just kept licking and stroking, and when I found a spot that had her hips shifting, grinding against my mouth, her lips parting, her moans slipping into the air, I arrowed in, put all my focus there.

"Raph," she whispered. "Fuck, honey. That's—"

I sucked on that spot on her labia.

"Fuck. I—oh, my *God*—" Her neck arched, head pressing back into the pillows.

And I kept going, sucking firmly and then darting my tongue to her clit, flicking and pressing there, bringing my thumb into the action so I could hit both her clit and that spot in tandem. Then I was barely in my own body at all, barely on the planet.

My next breath existed solely for the purpose of making this woman come.

Circles with my tongue. Suction with my mouth. Sliding into her tight wet heat with my finger. Fighting for control when her pussy clamped down hard.

"Honey." Her body jerked.

I pressed it in, slid it out, circling her entrance, pumping slow and steady and—

"*Honey.*"

Another jerk.

"More?" I asked against her.

Her breath caught. Her cheeks went pink.

But then she held my eyes and nodded.

I grinned, slid in again, this time with a second finger, both scissoring and curling, finding the movements that had her body jerking again, "Honey" tumbling from her lips, her neck arching and head pressing back into the pillow again.

Her pussy clenched, and she surprised the shit out of me by her hands coming to my head, fingers weaving into my hair, her hips bucking against my mouth.

In one second, it went from me being in control, slowly and carefully building her need, to her riding my face and fingers, fucking my face, her cheeks flushed, eyes closed, fingers tightly gripping my hair, as though she were worried that I would pull away.

I wouldn't.

I could be drowning, suffocating in her pussy, and I wouldn't pull away.

Not until she came apart on my mouth and fingers.

Not until she cried out my name.

Not until she was sated and limp and—

"Raph!"

I'd found a spot. A better one. Deep inside her pussy, and it had her shuddering, her pussy clamping, her back arching so that her tits popped free of the hem of that jersey. Hardened pink tips that called to my mouth, flesh that bounced and screamed for my hands.

I reached up, cupped her breast, molding it against my palm, running my thumb over her nipple.

"I'm—oh shit, baby. I'm going to—*don't stop.*"

I'd rolled her nipple between thumb and forefinger.

So I did it again, fingers still deep and rubbing that spot, mouth still working on her folds, thumb on her clit pinching and circling.

"Raph, fuck Raph. Oh, my God—"

And...thank fuck that was enough.

A gush of liquid on my fingers, dripping down my palm, her pussy clamping around my fingers, my name, long and drawn out on her tongue.

Her body taut, taut, *taut*...

And then limp, her back going flat, legs no longer clenching my head and shoulders, fingers slipping free of my hair, falling to the mattress.

She tilted her head to the side, lids barely open.

Her lips tilted up. "Raphael Gomez, you have got some fucking *skills*."

That had *my* lips tilting.

I leaned in, flicked out my tongue.

"Want to see them again?"

EIGHTEEN

Beth

"WANT TO SEE THEM AGAIN?"

I was limp and languid, barely coherent, but that silky question had desire pulsing through me. Yeah, I wanted to see those skills again. Those broad fingers were still inside me, and I could feel myself clenching around them, each pulse sending pleasure through me. His thumb was still near my clit, no longer pressing the hardened bud firmly, just gently circling, staying well away from the sensitive nerves so as not to over-stimulate me.

But it was encircling, and it was doing it gently and even though I'd just come, it was ramping me up again.

Now a brush over the top, over the apex of nerves.

My hips bucked.

His hand on my breast convulsed.

His eyes were deep blue, darkened with need, and when I managed to tear my gaze from them, from the beauty of his face —a sheen of sweat on his forehead, a dash of flush on his cheeks, stubble on his jaw, a muscle flickering as he pressed his lips together—I trailed it down his neck with its bobbing Adam's apple; his shoulders and chest, big and muscled and flexing; down to his abs, flat, no six-pack, but thick and strong and I totally wanted to trace my tongue over every inch of his bare skin. But mostly, I wanted to trail my tongue over the monster pressing against his boxer briefs.

So, the quiet question didn't have me taking him up on his offer.

It had me sitting up—and, oh boy, did that do nice things to the fingers inside me, the hand on my breast.

But I was a woman on a mission.

A mission I hadn't known I needed to complete until that moment.

My hands went to his shoulders, pushing him back.

Maybe I took him by surprise, maybe it was my mission that gave me super strength to move a bulky hockey player.

What that mission was?

Getting my mouth on his cock.

His fingers slipped free as I crawled over him, pressing him into the carpet, hands trailing along that strong chest, his flat abs, and...jerking down his boxers.

"Baby—" he began, but the words cut off the moment I squirmed down and my head dipped, taking him deep into my mouth.

He was big and hard and tasted salty.

Fucking delicious.

Fucking beautiful.

"Beth—"

He broke off on a groan when I swallowed him down, and since he liked that, I kept at it. Swallowing him deeper, bobbing and sucking hard, gripping him at his base, timing my strokes with flicks of my tongue up the underside, trailing it over his head.

A jerk of his hips had me focusing there.

Taking him deep, sucking him hard. Gripping the base, teasing his head.

I was pleasuring him, I was sucking his cock, and yet I was more turned on than I had *ever* been in my entire life.

His big body trembling beneath mine, his fingers in my hair, holding me steady, albeit with the occasional jerk of hips and hands telling me that his control was razor thin. I wanted to break it, wanted him to lose it, to fuck my mouth and come down my throat.

"Beth," he rasped, fingers flexing, trying to tug me off.

His thighs flexed beneath me, and I sensed his body getting ready to move. And I knew, I *knew* that I would be on my back in the next second, Raph over me, *in* me, taking me to new heights.

And this was where my newfound superhuman strength came in.

Hands sliding from my hair, he gripped my shoulders, pushing back lightly, his tone full of warning when he said, "Beth, honey, careful—"

Ignoring that press, I flexed my legs, holding tight around his thighs.

And then I dipped my head deeper, sucked him harder, stroked him faster.

"Fuck." A hiss. "Baby."

I set my tongue working.

"*Beth.* If you don't stop, honey, I'm going to—"

I groaned against his dick, and he made one more token protest, and then his hands weren't pushing me away.

They were bringing me closer.

Up and down. Gripping tight. Sucking deep. Tongue and just a little bit of teeth.

He shuddered—hips jerking, sending him down my throat.

But I just took what he was giving, was happy to take it all.

"Sugarpie, I'm—"

I moaned but didn't stop.

And then he shattered.

And...it was fucking glorious. I watched his eyes squeeze shut, his neck arch, his stomach flex, and then I was swallowing the hot spurts of his cum, choking on it, but dutifully taking as much as I could. Because it was Raph's. Because it tasted good. Because I needed it and the feel of it in my mouth, my throat was fucking hot.

When it stopped, I slowly slid him from my mouth, sucking lightly to get every last drop, and then when I finally released him, tongue sliding over the head, I licked my lips.

"Fuck, honey," he rasped. He was still hard in my hand, and his cock twitched as he curled up and rubbed his thumb over my bottom lip.

I nipped at his fingertip, loving when he groaned.

Then I was gasping out a little shriek when, one second he was beneath me, and the next I was in his arms, and the one after *that,* I was sitting on the bed. His fingers on the hem of the jersey I'd bought for him. A tug that had it over my head. A toss that sent it across the room.

Then my back was on the mattress and his mouth was on mine and he was kissing me like he didn't give a fuck that I'd just blown him.

Kissing me with an intensity that sent my already pulsing clit practically vibrating with need. Kissing me in a way that had me ready and wanting him deep. Kissing me so that I was wrapping my legs around him, arching up and rubbing my bare pussy against the hard length of his cock.

But he didn't hurry, even though I was on him, moaning into his mouth, desperate for him in an instant.

He kissed me until he was good and ready to be done, and then he slid his mouth along my jaw to my ear. "Good, baby?"

That had me grinning, even though my lungs were working like I'd run a 5K (and I fucking *hated* running). Orgasms, though. I didn't mind them. I'd be happy to be on the receiving end of Raph's fingers and tongue any day of the week. "Considering I have a big, sexy hockey player on top of me and we just exchanged mutually fulfilling orgasms?"

A grin.

A nip to my earlobe.

"Yeah, considering that."

I grinned, ran my fingers through his hair. "Considering all that, I'm great."

Laughter in his eyes.

Then they drifted down toward my chest, and I was never more thankful for this pregnancy than seeing how his face changed when he checked out my new and improved breasts. Of course, I'd been thanking the increased sensitivity that had made me practically come from just a finger and thumb roll earlier.

He lifted a hand, cupped one, thumb swiping over my nipple. "Would you be better if I spend some quality time with these?"

My smile widened. "Yeah, baby."

He didn't make me wait, didn't make me beg or even ask again.

He just bent and worshipped—yes, worshipped—my breasts. Nipples teased and breasts massaged. All light and delicate and then when I asked for it, thrust my hands into his hair and held him close, he gave me more.

More suction. More tongue. More teeth.

"Raph," I begged after he'd spent long minutes in no apparent hurry. His hands only on my breasts, not easing the ache between my legs, not touching me anywhere else.

Just driving me crazy.

"Raph, honey, I need—"

His head came up, eyes hot. "I know exactly what you need."

"Unless it's your cock in my pussy," I snapped, chest heaving, "then you're not a fucking mind reader, Raph."

He smirked, dropped his head again, sucking on a nipple. "It's my cock in your pussy."

Thank fuck.

He glanced up, still smirking. "So, I'm a mind reader, baby?"

He was. He was playing my body like he could read every thought running through my brain. But I wasn't going to admit that, so I just spread my legs and reached for his hips, trying to draw him down into me.

But he didn't drop his hips, just reached for his wallet on the nightstand and pulled out a condom.

"I can't get any more pregnant, honey," I murmured.

"I know," he said, tearing the packet open with his teeth and smoothing the condom down the hard length of his erection. "And I want to be in you without a condom. Believe me, I want that tight slick heat surrounding my cock, want to feel the wet that I had on my tongue on my dick. But you're turned on, same as me. You want this, same as me. And we've been dancing around this for too fucking long. So, honey, this isn't the time to have a conversation about condoms and STD tests and consent. It's the time to go slow and be smart and take precautions until we're ready to go there."

Raph was making sense.

I hated that.

But then the condom was on, and he was back on top of me, and his lips came to mine, the tip of his cock brushing my wet heat.

"Ready, honey?"

So *fucking* ready.

But the only answer I could give was wrapping one leg around his waist, drawing him to me as he pressed inside.

He was big and hard and heavy enough that I knew we'd have to get creative as my belly grew.

But...he was big and hard and inside me and—

"Raph," I breathed.

His eyes hit mine, and the demons howled. I knew he felt it, too. This was big and important and...different from everything that had come before, from everything that would come after.

"I know, sugarpie," he whispered when he was fully in, giving me a second to adjust before he began to move slow and steady and deep. That was...it was everything. His big body surrounding mine, his cock thrusting deep, his scent in my nose, his hands gentle on my body. "I know," he whispered again, and then he was moving faster, taking my mind off the fact that something had irrevocably shifted in me.

Cracked.

Unlocked.

Fell to the earthen floor.

I wasn't focused on that.

Because he was hard and deep and *in*. Because he was moving in a way that had my hips thrusting up to meet his, both of our bodies focused on a rhythm that would send us into the best kind of oblivion.

Because his lips were finding mine, and his tongue was darting into my mouth.

Because one hand was taking his weight, and the other was cupping one breast.

Because then that one hand slipped between us and found my clit.

Because that touch had me gasping, breaking the kiss, and bucking against him, my orgasm barreling down on him, the pleasure of it threatening to shatter me to pieces.

He arched, sucking at my nipple, hips still working, thumb still on me, and—

It hit with an impact that stole my breath.

A maelstrom of pleasure firing through my nerves, burning through my senses.

His name on my lips.

His body working mine, wringing every drop of pleasure before he began to lose his rhythm, before I managed to peel my lids open enough to watch his orgasm crash into him, take him down harder than a check on the ice.

It was beautiful watching that pleasure my body had given him, taking him down.

It was beautiful the way he kissed me after he'd finished.

It was beautiful how he rolled us and tucked me into his side, calloused fingers trailing over my naked skin.

And *that* was when I felt it.

The door in the basement shattered...and a dark, frightening demon slid out of the shadows and stepped into the light.

NINETEEN

Raph

I FELT Beth slip from the bed, the blankets shifting ever so slightly as she moved, and I wondered how in the fuck to play this.

Because we had made love, and it was the best sex of my life, and I'd been lying there in the throes of all that goodness, reliving every moment and adding things to my mental sex list left and right and she'd gotten increasingly tense against me.

Until I'd snapped out of the post-orgasm haze, and I'd started paying attention.

I knew it had been a bit for her and her body had changed, and she had lots of hormones flowing through her and we'd been dancing around this for a while, but when we'd moved, we moved *fast*. I'd thought she'd needed gentling, so I'd cuddled her closer, gentled my touches. I'd kissed her hair, murmured soft words. And all the while, she'd turned into a fucking statue against me.

Finally, I'd asked her if she was okay.

And she'd lied, faked the fakest yawn I'd ever heard in my life (and Monica had been party to numerous fake yawns, feigning fatigue like it was an Olympic sport), and had curled into me saying, "I'm just tired."

It was late.

Really late.

She was growing two babies after a stressful week.

She probably *was* tired.

But that wasn't what had her playing a statue after the best sex of my life, after we'd both come twice, after we'd shared something in this bed, and it was less to do with orgasms and more to do with actual feelings that were blooming.

At least in me.

Maybe the two orgasms were enough for her.

Maybe she was done with me.

Maybe—

The door to the bathroom clicked closed.

I rolled to the side, watched a band of light at the bottom of that wooden door appear.

Soft and sweet, gentle eyes and curved lips...turning into tense lines bracketing her mouth, eyes that wouldn't meet mine, a body that was turned into mine but wasn't holding me, was just there.

Next to me.

Not connected.

I lifted my hands to my eyes, dug my palms in. "Fuck," I whispered, realizing that I was totally out of practice with this shit, realizing that I both somehow knew Beth and yet didn't know her at all.

At. *All.*

Which meant I had no clue how to play this. Had it meant as much to her as it did me? Because of that, did she need space? Or did she need me to break through the walls she was trying to rebuild?

All questions I had no fucking answers to.

"Shit," I muttered, digging my palms in harder.

A noise in the bathroom had me freezing.

It wasn't the sink running or the toilet flushing. It wasn't the sound of the shower turning on.

It was—

I threw the sheets back, stood, and was across the room before I even fully processed what I was hearing. Because I *knew* what I was hearing. It sat heavy in my gut, squeezed my heart tight in a fist, throttling the organ, ripping, tearing, shredding my insides.

Then I was in the bathroom.

And she was...curled in a ball on the floor, her head in her hands.

And...she was sobbing.

Quietly, almost silently, but a steady stream of tears was pouring down her cheeks, her chest was shaking, and she was curled so tightly into that ball, rocking so fiercely that I was worried she was going to hurt herself.

I moved to her, started to reach for her, but she must have heard me, because she crammed herself back into the corner further. "No! Don't touch me!"

That had me freezing.

That had my outstretched hands halting, drawing back. "Beth, honey."

She pressed her forehead to her knees, tightened further. "Don't touch me. Don't touch me. Don't touch me."

"Beth," I whispered.

"Don't touch me. Don't touch—"

I knew I shouldn't touch her, *knew* it. But I also knew that she wasn't there, wasn't in that time, that moment. It was cold in the house, and she was sitting on the floor naked, and she was shaking so hard that I was worried she was going to hurt herself.

So, I went with my instincts.

Maybe wrong. Maybe stupid.

But...it was all I had in that moment.

I slipped my arms around her.

"Don't—"

"I have you." And I did, lifting her gently, carrying her back into the bedroom, tucking her into bed.

"Don't hurt me," she whispered.

I went still.

"Don't hurt me," she whispered again.

I cupped her cheeks. "Beth, honey. I won't hurt you. I promise."

Her eyes weren't focused, not on anything in the present. She was trapped somewhere deep, somewhere dark. "Don't hurt me. Please. I won't tell. I won't. I promise."

"Beth."

Her eyes hit mine, but they were still unfocused, and she shoved out of the bed, hit the floor, body bending on itself again. "I promise. I *promise* I won't tell the demons. I won't let them out. I won't. I won't. I *won't*—"

Fuck.

This was...I didn't know how to deal with this.

I stood up, grabbed the jersey from the floor, tugging it over her head, covering her body, trying to keep her warm in the cool house. A yank had the blanket from the bed, and I wrapped it around her.

"Beth, honey. It's Raph. You're here with me now. You're safe. I promise."

She quieted, but didn't come back to me, just huddled in

that blanket, rocking lightly back and forth, back and forth, back and forth.

"Can you talk to me, honey? Tell me what's wrong?"

Her forehead pressed to her knees; her arms wrapped tighter. "The demons are trying to escape. They'll hurt everyone, ruin everything. I can't let them out. I can't let them out. I can't—"

"I'm here with you," I said gently, moving closer, carefully peeling her hand free, lacing our fingers together. "I can help you with the demons. I can—"

Her head jerked off her knees, eyes wide and wild and *still not here*. "They'll hurt you. They'll hurt you. They'll—"

"I'm strong, sugarpie."

Just rocking. Just repeating that they would hurt me over and over again.

I carefully peeled her other hand free, slowly, gently, incrementally brought her into my side. "I'm here. You're okay," I whispered in answer to those chanted words that had no context in the now, in this moment, from the woman I'd come to know.

But it didn't break through, didn't bring her back to me.

And as I held her, as she sat on the floor, rocking and shivering and not herself, I hated to do it.

Hated that I couldn't make this go away.

Hated that this wasn't a moment I could just hold her and talk to her and make everything okay.

This was...deep and heavy, and I didn't have one fucking clue how to handle it.

So I hated to do it, but I also didn't know what else to do.

Keeping my arms around her, that soft chant slicing through me, I reached to the side, snagged my pants, and pulled out my cell.

Then I called the one person I thought might be able to help.

Hazel.

TWENTY

Beth

I WOKE up in a bed that wasn't mine.

The lights were off, but it was brighter than my bedroom, illumination from beeping machines and a large glass door seeping into the room.

The bed was small.

The blanket and sheets were hospital grade.

I had tubes and wires hooked up to me.

Had I—

I tried to think back. I'd been in bed with Raph after we'd had sex. Sex that was so fucking incredible and mind-altering, and I'd loved it so much that though I'd been a puddle of limp satiated woman, I'd been trying to summon the energy to attack him again.

To taste him.

To take a ride atop all that yummy hockey player.

To—

"Beth?"

I blinked, turning my head, and even that little bit of movement was painful, as though every single muscle in my body had been used until it was burned out, like I'd been to the most tortuous fitness class on the planet, and then done it again, just for funsies.

Oh, God.

I stared up into Raph's bright blue eyes.

"The babies?" I asked.

Or rather, rasped, because fuck, my throat was dry.

Something flittered across his face—relief, anger, fear, I couldn't tell. But he reached for a pitcher on the rolling table, poured some water into a cup, and opened the straw. "The babies are fine." He bent the straw and brought it to my mouth, inclining his head to one of the beeping monitors. "That's tracking their heartbeats, and your ultrasound looked great."

I drank deeply.

Then he set the cup down and lifted a strip of ultrasound pictures from the table, holding them up so I could see.

My heart skipped a beat.

They were okay.

I was okay.

"What happened?" I whispered.

"I was kind of hoping you could tell me that."

Pushing my hair back, I tried to weave my way through the fog in my mind. "We were in bed, honey."

"Yeah." A gentle prompt.

"And we'd finished..." My cheeks went hot. "I...it was good. Really good, and I was trying to summon the energy to attack you again."

That had his lips turning up.

But he didn't say anything. He just waited for me to speak again, and I did my best to wind my way through the blackness of my memories. What the hell had happened?

"You got stiff, sugarpie," he said softly. "Then went into the bathroom."

My stomach began sinking. "I did?"

"Yeah, honey."

Shit.

What had I—?

The sliding glass door *whirred* open, and I jerked my head to the side—and God that hurt—to see Hazel moving into the space, a woman in a pale blue sweater and a badge around her neck trailing behind her.

Oh no.

Now my stomach was twisting itself into knots.

"Raph," I whispered. "Wh-what happened?"

"Sugar—"

"*Raph.*" Panic began squeezing my insides. "What did I do to you?"

"Nothing," he said. "I'm fine."

This didn't seem like nothing. Being in a hospital bed with tubes in my hands, machines beeping around me, and Hazel and Raph and the woman with the badge all staring at me in concern. Definitely not *nothing*. This was—

"Breathe, honey," Hazel said gently, closing the distance between us and weaving our fingers together. "Everything is okay. The babies are good. You're good. Raph is good. This is my friend Marin Stewart. She's a licensed clinical social worker and we're going to step out so you can talk to her."

Oh, God.

Hazel was using her gentle voice.

Her Beth-is-going-to-lose-her-shit, or maybe her Beth-had-already-lost-it voice.

Jesus Christ.

What had I done?

"No," I said, hand squeezing Hazel's. "Don't leave. Please.

I'm fine. I'm sure this was all just stress and fatigue and pregnancy—"

"And PTSD," Hazel murmured.

"I—" I clamped my lips together. "What?" I breathed. "That's not—" A shake of my head. "I'm not—I'm fine." I forced a smile. "It was just—"

Raph squeezed my hand. "You were shaking and begging me not to hurt you."

Oh, fuck.

"I was there for the nightmare, honey, and I let that slide, thinking I wasn't in a place to demand anything from you." He touched my jaw. "But, fuck, baby. I can't let this slide. You need to talk to someone about what's going on, and we need to get you the help you need—whether that's from me or Hazel or Marin."

"I'll be fine. I'm just—"

"You spent an hour huddled into a ball, not in the present, but somewhere dark."

The basement.

Fuck. *Fuck.* I was fucking up. Fucking this up, fucking up the good I was supposed to be giving.

Then my gaze caught on the window.

And the light shining through it.

"What time is it?" I whispered.

"Just after ten," Hazel supplied when Raph didn't answer.

I jerked my hand free. He had practice today, and he should be there. Not here. Not then. Not *ever.* "You've got to go."

Raph rocked back in his seat. "What?"

"You've got to get to the rink. You've got to go to work. You can't be here."

"I'm not going anywhere."

The monitors began beeping faster.

"You have to go." I whipped toward Hazel. "You both have to go. You can't see—" I clamped my teeth together. "You need to go. You need to *go. Go!*"

Marin straightened, and I didn't miss her glancing out the sliding door, probably looking for a doctor or nurse, someone who would give me something to calm down.

But I didn't want to take something to calm down, I didn't want to lose more hours.

This couldn't happen.

I had to lock down the doors. Shore off the basement.

Not let anyone in. No. Not let Raph and Hazel in.

"You both have work. I'm fine. I had a moment. I had—"

"Hours of not being in the present, sweetheart," Hazel murmured. "Hours of being trapped somewhere bad and not being aware of your body, not being able to communicate, not being able to tell everyone what was going on."

I knew it.

I'd felt it after, when I'd cuddled close.

Felt the demon slither free.

I should have acted then, but I'd been in that moment, relaxed and happy and with Raph, and so I hadn't prepared, hadn't been ready for the sneak attack, having expected it to come later, when I was alone.

That was when it always happened.

That was when the nightmares came, and I lost time, and—

That was when the demons of my past struck.

This wasn't the time to go down this path. It was pretty much the worst-case scenario for me in this moment. I needed to do damage control. I needed to save this somehow. I needed —distraction and avoidance and a shit ton of concrete to pour into the basement.

A deep breath. Another. The beeping on the monitors slowing.

Marin calming, her head turning back to me, concern still there, but less urgency.

Right. I had to get this done.

I turned to Raph. "The season is starting to wind down. This is an important time, and the playoffs are right around the corner. You can't miss a practice. The team needs you, and even if you leave right now, you'll already be late."

"Beth—"

I shoved at his shoulder, lost a bit of my cool exterior, even though I was trying desperately to hold tight to it. "You need to go. Like *right* now."

"I've already called Coach," he said, losing a bit of *his* cool. "So, table that shit right now. And even if the game is my job, and it's important, it's not as important as the people in my life." His eyes hit mine, held. "And I think I made it clear that you're important, and you're in my life, and I want to stay."

He had made that clear.

Not with words.

But then again, I hadn't needed them.

Because he'd made his feelings clear with actions.

With shopping and strawberry toast. Making sure I was safe in the bathroom and giving me water bottles. Mouthing *sugarpie* through the glass and his gentle fingers on my body. Through all of that and more, he'd made it certain that I knew his feelings had shifted.

That was why I'd bought the jersey.

That was why I'd been determined to take care of him in return—no, not in *return*, but bigger, better, to give him what he couldn't accept himself. To make him better and take away his pain.

Not to lay my baggage at his feet.

Not to make him worry and panic after we'd—

A sharp slice of embarrassment cutting through my middle,

heating my skin, making it feel like it was too small for my body. "You need to go," I whispered and then when I saw the protest that was building in his face, ready to slide loose in his words, I held his eyes. "You made it clear." A breath. "I know that. I feel that." So deeply that he'd prowled through my castle walls, traipsed through the basement, opening doors left and right. "But what I need from you now is to go."

His expression clouded.

"Beth, honey—" Hazel began.

"I need you to go, too." I tore my eyes from Raph's, turned to squeeze my friend's hand. "I know what you saw, and I understand what happened. And"—I swallowed hard—"I know what it means, what all this has dredged up." Hazel's brows dragged together, and I gave, just a little, just *the* little that Hazel already knew. "My mom. My stepdad," I whispered. "I think all of this"—I waved a hand—"the hospital, the complications, has dredged everything up."

"Honey."

"I'm not saying my head is right. But, right at this moment, I need some space to think and to talk to Marin and to figure out where it is and how to get it right again." I turned back to Raph. "So, what I'm asking, is for you guys to give me that space. Give me some time."

Raph's jaw was tight.

Hazel, when I glanced back, didn't look much better.

I knew that it wasn't in either of their repertoires to let this go without solving the problem, without fixing it.

What they didn't know, couldn't ever know, was that I was unfixable.

I was broken inside, had been for years and years.

Starting with that night, continuing over the years. Pieces broken again and again and *again.*

And at some point, no matter how many times they were

picked up and glued back together, there were always parts missing.

Important parts.

Lucky for me, I was good at faking things, at wearing a mask and making it believable that I was totally okay.

That I had it together.

I was Beth Mason, born with a silver spoon, a trust fund big enough that I could buy half of Manhattan if I wanted.

And a past full of demons.

Of pain.

Of memories and a truth that meant I could never, *ever* have anyone know the real me.

But in that moment, Hazel and Raph bought it.

"Okay, honey," Hazel whispered, slipping her hand free and brushing a kiss to my temple. "I'll call you in a couple of hours, and we'll get you home."

"Are Pru and—"

"Pru's still scouting. Marcel is at practice. We didn't tell them about the panic attack, just that you were dizzy again. I'm sure they'll be by later."

More penance I needed to pay.

"I *am* okay."

Hazel smiled. "I know, honey. Talk soon."

And then she was gone.

Unfortunately, Raph was there.

"I'm sorry I scared you," I whispered, struggling to keep my gaze on his.

"Don't apologize." His eyes flicked to Marin then back to mine, voice dropping. "If you don't want to talk to her, I'll find—"

I didn't want to talk to Marin. I didn't want to talk to *anyone.*

But I wasn't going to get out of this without talking to *someone.*

So...I'd talk to Marin.

I'd say what I needed to say, give enough that I could get the fuck out of here, and then I would lock my shit down, make sure Raph was good and solid, and then I would find him a woman he could love and trust and be with.

Even if that meant setting me aside.

No, because that *would* mean setting me aside.

Because that was the right path for Raph.

And it just so happened to be the right path for me.

TWENTY-ONE

Raph

IT HAD TAKEN everything in me to walk out of that room, and I knew it had been just as hard for Hazel when she came close the moment the door slid closed behind me.

I wrapped my arm around her as we moved to the elevators, waiting until we were inside to order, "Tell me."

"Her stepdad and mom had a very...tumultuous relationship."

Yeah, well, clearly that was the understatement of the year, considering what had happened over the last couple of hours.

I released a breath, trying to control my temper. "He hurt her."

That wasn't said as a question, but Hazel still took my words as one.

"I don't think so," she said carefully as the elevator doors closed. "I do know there was a lot of yelling and things were so intense that she was happy to be living at school instead of at home, even though both of us were way too young to be living on our own."

"He *hurt* her," I repeated.

This time with an emphasis on *hurt* so Hazel knew it was fact and not a question.

Hazel blinked, glanced up at me. "She tell you that?"

"She had a nightmare after that night in the ER, crying out and begging him not to hurt her."

Hazel's eyes went wide. "Shit," she whispered.

If she hadn't told Hazel about that, hadn't told her and Pru, then how deep was this shit buried? And what hope did I have of digging it out, of helping her slay those demons she was talking about? Because it was clear they needed to be obliterated, to be destroyed, but...she didn't even want me in the room.

The elevator began moving down.

Hazel turned in the circle of my arm and stared up at me.

There was fire in her brown eyes. "I need to know that you're in this."

I blinked. What the fuck?

She squeezed my hand. "You need to know where your head is at because if what you suspect is true, that means she's had twenty-five years to bury it deep, and we've got a long road ahead of us to dig it out."

I shook my head. "Hazel—"

She poked me in the chest, her tone more intense than I'd ever heard it. Usually, she was soft and gentle, guiding the guys through their shit without pushing (though she had a spine of steel and definitely *would* push as needed). But this—the jab in my chest, the sharp tone—wasn't typical Hazel, and it immediately had me even more on edge.

Because if Hazel was concerned enough to lose her normal calm edge, then this was some dark, dark stuff.

"Monica hurt you," she said. "She made you question everything you'd built and trusted, and that cuts deep. I care about you, the guys care about you, which should be obvious considering the way they closed ranks when she tried to get to you."

Monica *had* tried to weasel back in.

The guys *had* closed ranks.

And yeah, Monica had hurt me, but mostly, I was realizing, I'd hurt myself. My parents weren't great—my dad spent most of his time yelling and bitching about his life being shit, and my mom was flighty and weak and unreliable and hadn't been any kind of barrier between me and my dad's anger, and then she'd peaced out altogether, leaving me to deal with all that anger. I had been—obviously because of all that rockiness—gun shy when it came to diving into something serious. So, I hadn't dated seriously, just fucked around and had fun, and relied on my instincts to choose right when the time came. And I'd thought that time had come when I asked Monica out.

Beautiful. Sweet. A good job. A life put together.

I'd trusted myself to have finally chosen right.

And even when I'd considered moving on because there wasn't a big spark, my feelings for her weren't growing like I'd wanted, I'd still thought I could trust myself.

Because she might not be forever.

But I'd chosen right.

Not my parents. Not someone toxic. Someone good that any man would be lucky to have, just not me being that man.

Then when she was pregnant, I thought that the spark would grow, that she was a good choice and a good woman, and *my instincts* told me we could make a good go of it.

I was moving forward.

Being smart.

Using the good examples of relationships around me to create something good for myself, to create a family that was mine and healthy and something I really, *really* wanted.

But...I'd chosen poorly.

My instincts had led me to make the shittiest decision of all.

And I'd gotten fucked in the process.

But I didn't have a chance to tell Hazel all of that, all of what I'd realized, that I was finally understanding why it had taken me over a year to sort my head—because me choosing Monica, me not seeing her for what she was meant I'd managed to shake the foundation of everything that was inside me, what made me *me* and...

Well, I didn't get a chance to tell her any of that because her voice was gentling and her hand was on my arm, and her eyes were earnest...and she was still talking. "And yeah, I know my job with the team is to be the resident head-getter-together, and I know you know I saw that you were hurting. But I also knew the guys were close, and because you've been playing out of your mind, because you were functioning and hadn't asked for help, I haven't waded in, haven't forced you to face it."

The elevator doors opened.

"And maybe I should have."

We stepped off, but we didn't immediately head for the hospital exit.

Instead, Hazel snagged my arm and tugged me to the side, glancing around to make sure no one was within earshot before going on. "I thought you were slowly sorting out your shit, so I've been keeping an eye on you, watching close, making sure that you were moving in the right direction."

I sucked in a breath, started to reply again, but she kept going.

"And, good grief, it was taking a *long* time, but because I thought you were slowly inching forward, I was waiting.

Watching. Making sure you were still moving but trying to give you the space to do it on your own terms because you're a big, broody hockey player and I know I can only push you guys so far." A small smile. "And plus, you were playing good and living, and I didn't want to set you back when I wasn't sure I could help yank you forward."

That, despite the circumstances, had me wanting to grin.

"So maybe I was stupid and shouldn't have let you play this out slowly, shouldn't have thrown Beth into your path just because I thought you guys would be good together and I knew she liked you, knew she would be good for you because she's an awesome woman and friend." Her eyes filled with tears. "But I didn't know she was hiding this." A breath. "And this is big, Raph. This is really freaking big, and you've been really, really hurt, and I can't guarantee she won't hurt you and that you won't hurt her and that this won't blow up in your faces and—"

"Hazel."

She closed her eyes, inhaled, and exhaled slowly. "What I walked into in her room last night is heavy enough, buried deep enough that she didn't share it with me, and I've known her almost her entire life, and we've shared a lot of heavy." Her lids opened, revealing damp brown eyes. "It's heavy in a way that I'm not sure *I* can handle, let alone a man who has been hurt in a heavy and deep way all on his own, a way I would totally get at balking at taking on something like this."

I'd been with Hazel throughout the entire conversation, understanding her, respecting her, appreciating the way she'd handled my situation and Beth's, glad she'd brought in someone who would get Beth the help she needed.

But the last pissed me off.

"She's not something to *take on*," I snapped, stepping closer. "She's a beautiful woman who I've wanted for years.

Someone funny and caring and kind, and you should know that, considering she's been your best friend for fucking *years*."

"Raph—"

"Does she wear a ton of shields, some of which I'm just starting to be able to peek around, and most of which are probably still buried deep? Fuck, yes."

"Raph—"

"But does the way she smiles, how thoughtful she is, the person she is beneath the surface and who I suspect she is below all those shields mean that I would walk through fire for her? Fuck, yes." I scowled. "And there is no hesitation on my part because I spent a lifetime not knowing the difference between a good woman and a bad one, between a shit relationship and a good one. Because I've realized that what threw me for so big a fucking loop with Monica is not because she was a bitch—and newsflash, she was—but because *I* chose her. I trusted myself to have finally picked something good, and she wasn't that."

Now Hazel's face softened. "Raph."

"So my bullshit is my bullshit, and I didn't even get exactly what it was until five minutes ago. That being said"—I straightened—"I'm going to think that shit through, make sure it doesn't color my life going forward because Beth, *Beth* fucking deserves a man with his head on straight, who'll go to bat for her, even when shit swirls. And I know"—I jabbed a finger in her direction—"that *you* know that's true because Beth is *Beth,* and though I've only known her for three years and you've known her for almost a lifetime, she's *Beth.*"

Silence.

So I clipped out, "Don't have anything to say to *that?*"

Her lips tipped up. "Was just waiting to make sure you were done." She snagged my hand, leaned against my arm. "That was quite a roll you were on there."

"Any of it wrong?"

Her head plunked onto my shoulder. "Nope. Beth is Beth and she's worth digging deep and staying close for the long run." A beat. "And that means forever, Raph. Just in case you were wondering how long you needed to have your mind straight for."

"You think I finally got it together to falter at the finish line?"

Hazel lifted her head. "I think that you're a good man and Beth has had some stuff go down, stuff that's cut through the fog around you and prompted you into motion."

I felt my scowl start again.

"And that's a good thing. I'm glad you're here and glad that you got your head right." A breath, tone bordering on careful. "But you're a man of action, you're a man who likes fixing things and being the person to make things right. And I know Beth is that way, too. I know you can both help each other."

"But?"

"But I don't much believe in miraculous left turns when it comes to trauma. It takes work to get through that, and even though you might have all the answers in this moment, in the future..."

"It took me a year to get to this point—"

"A point you only recognized five minutes ago."

Well, fuck. As much as it annoyed me, she was right.

"I'm not leaving her," I said stubbornly.

"I hope you won't," Hazel whispered. "I just..." She squeezed my arm again. "Just keep working through that puzzle in that head of yours, and if it gets too heavy or you're suddenly missing a few pieces, talk to me or Smitty or one of the guys."

"Smitty's got a big mouth," I muttered.

"So, me."

"You'll just tell Ollie."

"I wouldn't. You know that." Not offended, amusement in those brown eyes. Amusement led to a beatific smile. "Talk to Beth then."

I shook my head. "She's got enough on her plate."

"And knowing Beth like I do—though clearly that knowledge has some holes in it considering the events of the last few hours." She made a face. "Anyway, the point is that nothing makes a woman like Beth feel like herself so much as being needed and part of something." Hazel's expression went a little stark, eyes unseeing, giving the impression of looking into the past...and her next words proved I was right. "Take it from a former boarding school kid who spent a lot of time trying to find where she fit and what useful role she could play," she said softly before giving me a nudge, belying the serious words, taking the edge off with an easy smile. "Or take it from looking into *yourself*. I think you know something about having a mission and how that gives you a way of focusing on what's important."

I knew that Hazel was right.

I still shot her a glare.

Mostly, because she was right.

But also, because I didn't like all of what she'd said, especially that shit about finding her place. She was an integral part of the Breakers, and we would be much worse without her... and frankly, *I* would be worse without her.

I was lucky to call her a friend.

"You're important to the team," I said. "You have to know that you're one of the most important pieces."

She giggled. "I think the actual players on the ice, playing the actual games could make an argument against that."

"Hazel," I growled. "*You're* important."

Her hand squeezed my shoulder, smile widening. "Your protective streak is showing."

Damn right it was.

But I had the feeling that nothing would make her feel so much as a show of the Raph I used to be, the old Raph I felt bubbling just beneath the surface. "You know," I said, tapping a finger to my chin as we moved toward the exit. "I haven't been feeling much like myself for the last while."

"Yeeeah," she said carefully, drawing out the agreement in a way that had me smiling.

"Which means that I haven't really spent much time doing my favorite pastime."

"I don't want to hear about your sex life."

I burst out laughing as we walked out the double doors, and *God* that felt good. "I was talking about pranks, Haze. Lots and lots of pranks are in yours and the boys' futures."

She groaned. "I take it back."

"What back?"

"Don't sort out your head. Stay stuck in it so I don't have to deal with another round of Someone's Superglued a Body Part to Something."

I nudged her. "Now you're just giving me ideas."

Another groan, her head tipping back. "Dear God. I work with children. Big, burly ones who are giant pains in my asses."

A tug of her ponytail. "You love it. Now," I said when she lifted her head, but didn't argue my point, "am I driving you home, or is Oliver coming to get you?"

Her face gentled and she nodded to the right. "He's waiting in the lot."

I approved. "I'll walk you over."

"Okay," she murmured.

But we didn't get very far because then Ollie was there, his gait so steady, no one would have guessed it was done on one prosthetic leg, never mind that it was recent and had ended his career.

Fuck.

Ollie had his head straight. He understood his priorities and all the good that came from having a woman like Hazel.

My shit was hardly in the same realm as Oliver's.

So I needed to make doubly sure mine was shoveled away, that I was ready to be there for Beth.

Because I had some motherfucking demons to slay.

TWENTY-TWO

Beth

MARIN WAS STANDING NEXT to the hospital bed, clipboard in her hand and pressed to her belly.

And she was silent.

Studying me.

Raph and Hazel were gone, slipping through the sliding door, leaving me with Marin. And now I needed to figure out how to play this.

What to give.

How to find some peace.

"That was masterfully done."

My eyes had been on the clear blue plastic of the clipboard, the label declaring it property of the emergency department, small silver rivets on the back, but Marin's dry sentence had my eyes shooting up.

She was a clipboard thief.

So none of what Marin said in that moment meant anything.

Right. Nice attempt at an argument.

"I don't know what you're talking about," I said quietly.

Another attempt at an argument—pretending to know nothing.

Marin fell silent then, still and silent and studying me like I was a puzzle and she knew exactly where all the pieces went.

But I already knew so many of the pieces were lost and missing that what was inside me wouldn't ever make a complete picture.

"Don't you?" Marin pressed softly, moving to the bed, and leaning a hip to the edge.

"No," I said, holding tight to the argument. "I don't."

"Hmm."

An inhale held for a long moment. Then an exhale going on for just as long.

"You're not going to give me anything, are you?"

My chin came up, and I struggled to keep my tone even. "I'm not stupid. I know what happened wasn't good or normal, so I'm happy to talk to you."

Piercing gray eyes on mine. "Or you'll give me just enough to get me to back off so that you can go back to"—air quotes here—"normal."

Marin was good at her job.

But I wasn't going to admit anything.

"You might get that normal back, Beth. Hell"—respect in her eyes—"you strike me as a survivor, so I'm guessing that you probably *will* get it back. At least for a little while," she added, with such certainty that my gut twisted. "But sooner or later," Marin went on. "Sooner or later, this is going to happen again. You can't bottle everything up forever and expect it to not eventually work itself free again."

I could damned well try.

I could carry these babies and help Raph and get the fuck out of Baltimore before it happened again.

"But I saw you come in..."

My hands clenched into fists.

Which Marin saw, if the way her gaze darted there was any indication.

Bitch.

I meant that in the nicest way possible, meant it to be a self-protective shield because all I wanted was to get the fuck out of this hospital and get away from Marin, and to go back to fucking *normal*...

Marin's face was placid. "I know I'm not going to get through those walls in one day, in a few hours. And I know that me knowing Hazel—"

"You can't tell Hazel anything," I snapped. "It's patient-client privilege."

Half of Marin's mouth curved. "No, I can't. And I wouldn't. But that wouldn't matter, anyway. Me knowing Hazel means that I would *never* get through your walls, would I?"

Fuck.

My outburst was stupid. It wasn't *normal*. It revealed too much.

And Marin knew it.

"So, I know I won't get in there. Just like I know that people don't have the kind of trauma you do without it being something big. So even though you won't let me in, won't let *them* in"—a wave to the glass door through which Hazel and Raph had disappeared—"even though you obviously have some things twisted in that head of yours, I'm begging—*begging*—you to keep these"—she pulled two cards out of her pocket and slid them onto the rolling table—"or at least keep *one* of them close and to use it when the time comes."

My eyes slanted down, and I studied the business cards.

One was Marin's, a bunch of letters following her name. The other was for another trauma therapist.

Fuck.

"And I'll say this before I sign off on the doctor discharging you and leave you to it. Aside from keeping them close"—a nod to the cards—"aside from *using* one of them when that darkness ramps again, preferably *before* it ramps again, I want you to know that everyone deserves to be happy." A beat. "Even those who think, for some reason, they don't."

Such simple words.

But they struck hard and true.

True enough that I couldn't hold Marin's gaze, that my eyes drifted away, and I became a fucking master at studying the stitching on the thin hospital-grade blanket. One stitch, two, three, more.

"Everyone," Marin whispered.

And then I heard the whoosh of the door, felt the quiet descend as it shut behind Marin.

My gaze lifted...to the cards on the table.

My stomach roiled.

But I didn't reach for them, didn't register the names.

I just left those rectangles of cardstock where they were and closed my eyes.

And because I was alone, I allowed it to happen...

Allowed a tear that was burning behind my eyelids to escape.

Just one.

One tear. One life. One woman who was broken and would never be whole.

"I KNOW IT'S INSANITY," Pru said softly, two days later, sitting next to me at her kitchen table. "But I just..."

I smiled gently. "Mila reminded you of you."

A nod. "We've been on the foster parent list for so long, we didn't expect to get a call, or for that call to fit, especially with the twins coming. Especially not bringing in a kid with a disease that we don't really know much about."

I reached over, squeezed Pru's hand. "You'll learn."

"I know we will. Because, God, she's only been here a couple of days and I'm in love." They had gotten the call while I had been getting discharged—which had served the dual purpose of giving a girl and Pru and Marcel something good in the form of an instant family, *and* getting me some space while everyone settled in. I'd settled their worry, hung at home, thankful my job was remote, not that I needed to work.

I didn't need the money, and I knew my boss would give me time off if I asked.

But I had to get back to normal.

Had to erase the worry Raph had in his eyes every time he looked at me.

Thank God he'd had a game the night before.

Because he'd hovered over me, him and Hazel both, that first day, and I'd been worried to say the wrong thing, to do the wrong thing, to trigger them or myself and...well, it hadn't been the most relaxing day of my life.

I needed more space, more time, more air to breathe and memories to squash, and luckily, we'd only had the morning together before he'd had to leave to go to the rink. When he'd left, I'd kept busy—organizing my closets, finishing a couple of projects for work, making cookies, and texting Raph regular updates, as he'd requested. Then later, I'd crawled into bed and watched the Breakers kick ass. Raph had played well as always, so I didn't need to add any hockey game guilt to my heavy bucket of it, thankfully, and then after, he'd come to my place again (though this time without the post-game side of thigh-high boots, his jersey, and incredible sexy time).

He'd slid into my bed, tugged the blankets over us, and held me.

And we hadn't talked about what had happened, hadn't talked about anything important—we'd just discussed the game and how I was feeling and Smitty being Smitty in the locker room.

It was like we were on a casual date with random chitchat.

It was weird.

It was...nice.

I liked being with Raph—minus being the cause of the shadows beneath his eyes—liked him holding me and sleeping next to him (though I didn't sleep well either night, mostly because I was worried that if I relaxed too much again, if I wasn't disciplined, those doors would open again and I would be right back where I'd begun)

This afternoon he had a charity event, so I'd cooked him lunch, saw him off, all the while doing anything and everything to convince him I was fine and coping with what had happened.

He was worried.

But I'd get him to understand it was a one-off.

"I'm in love and she's—" Pru cleared her throat, eyes a little glassy.

I squeezed my friend's hand. "Mila is special."

And she'd been alone.

An orphan who had sad eyes and a quiet disposition.

But Marcel and Pru had taken the classes. They had a bedroom always at the ready.

And now they had a little girl sleeping in the bed they'd so carefully picked out, having gone to a half-dozen stores before they'd made the purchase.

"Yeah," Pru whispered. "Really special."

"And you'll make her happy," I said.

"Yeah, I will."

I grinned. "And take her on lots of adventures that will turn Marcel's hair gray?"

Pru smiled now, the tension and heavy dissipating. "Exactly." But then insecurity slid back in. "Are we crazy?"

"Fuck yeah, you are," I teased. "But you're speaking to a woman who's raving with pregnancy hormones and craving Double-Stuffed Oreos, so you know...*c'est la vie*. You deserve a life that's full and happy, and so does she."

"Yeah, she does."

"And"—I punched Pru lightly on the arm—"you'll give it to her. I know you will, same as these babies will be happy and perfect and drive you absolutely bonkers because they're your eggs"—Pru had lost most of her reproductive parts, but she'd had one ovary, enough to harvest the eggs that had been implanted into me—"but they'll also probably be angels most of the time because it's Marcel's sperm."

Pru grinned.

"So, yes, it's crazy and I'm sure it will be overwhelming on most days and just a lot on others." Another punch. "But you two are the people I know most in the world who can handle it, who have so much love to give that they won't want for anything."

"Shit," Pru muttered.

"What?"

"I'm a badass former hockey player."

"Yeah, you are."

Pru wrinkled her nose. "And badass former hockey players aren't supposed to turn into blubbering fools just because one of their two best friends in all the world is freaking awesome and gushy."

"Meh." A shrug. "You could use a little gushiness."

Pru grinned. "Well, I know you'd give it to me, even if I *didn't* want it."

I grinned back. "Damn right I would."

"Okay." Pru smacked her hands on the table. "Now that you've given me the gushy you think I need—"

"*Know* you need," I chimed in.

Pru rolled her eyes. "Then you need to let me give you the gushy back."

Oh, God. I was holding it together. Gushy from the not-gushy Pru might crack the layers of concrete I was busy slathering on. "Pru, honey—"

"I never thought I could be this happy," my friend said. "But you and Hazel straightened my shit out so that I could see Marcel for what he was to me, and you..." Pru got a little choked up. "I know I've thanked you too many times already—"

"So just stop already," I whispered, my throat tight.

"But I'm not going to forget what you did for me then, and I won't forget it now or ever. So, you're going to shut up and let me tell you that I love you and that I really, *really* want you to find your own happy."

I inhaled.

"And just saying, I think Raph could make a woman happy. *Really* happy," she added with a curve of her lips. "Like *forever* happy."

A snake coiled in my belly, a demon poised at the door—

"Pru," I warned.

"And just saying—and Hazel agrees—you could make him happy back."

I swallowed hard. "*Pru.*"

My friend just smiled.

So, I gave her the rest, reaching across the table and gripping my friend's fingers. "I'm going to try."

"Good." Pru squeezed my hand back. "Because I know you won't just try, you'll do."

"Okay, Yoda."

A twitch of lips, a flash of white teeth. "Damn right." She pushed to her feet, headed for a cupboard. "Now, because you're carrying my babies and because Marcel and I both pay attention, you'll need to do us a favor and"—she opened a cupboard—"help us eat all of the Oreos."

I started laughing when I saw the entire cabinet was full of cookies, all double-stuffed.

"If you have milk," I teased, "then I think I can take care of at least half of those."

Pru laughed and went to retrieve the milk and two glasses, my friend's laughter filling a place deep in my belly.

But it didn't fill the basement.

Didn't cement the halls and stalls and the stairway.

Didn't add another layer of protection to make sure the demons didn't escape.

No matter how many cookies I ate, no matter how much milk I drank, no matter how many times I laughed with my friends, *it* was always there.

Burning through me.

Just like that card from Marin was burning a hole in my pocket.

TWENTY-THREE

Raph

I STROLLED up the front walk of Pru and Marcel's place, knocking lightly on the door.

Not wanting to disturb because they had a new kid to get settled in their house.

Mila Rose.

A pretty name.

I was looking forward to meeting her.

But...I needed to see Beth more.

Two days I'd spent not pushing. Two days I'd spent trying to calm the worry, to assure myself that she was okay. Two days I'd spent internalizing my shit, making sure my head was straight, that I'd taken what I'd learned about myself, what Hazel had told me to heart.

Two days when it had taken me two minutes.

I'd gotten my head out of my ass when Beth had passed out.

The events that followed had just served to reinforce I was on the right path.

But I'd wanted to be sure, and she deserved for me to be that way.

I was.

And I was done thinking about it.

Now had come the time for action.

The door swung open, and Beth stood there, surprise giving way to pleasure as her red lips parted in a wide smile. "Hey," she said, leaning close and rising on tiptoe, wrapping her arms around my shoulders. Her mouth hit my cheek, mostly because the moment she'd started reaching for me, I'd bent and closed the distance between us, making the contact happen.

"Hey, sugarpie," I murmured, her obvious happiness at seeing me settling deep inside my heart.

She dropped back onto her heels, smiling up at me. "What are you doing here?"

"Seeing you."

"I thought we'd meet up after I was done with—"

I reached forward, smoothed my thumb along her top lip. "You've got—"

I held it up, showed her the black crumbs I'd just wiped off.

"Oh," she whispered on a shaky breath. Then she shrugged and her mouth turned up. "Double-Stuffed Oreos are my weakness."

I filed that knowledge away for future reference—along with mentally ordering several giant ass boxes of the cookie sandwiches—then slid my hand down her arm and laced our fingers together. "I didn't want to wait to see you." Her lips parted on an exhale and I pressed my lips to her forehead. "Your night was okay?"

"It was good. *Really* good. Mila is sweet, and Pru and Marcel are in love."

"Good," I murmured.

"Do you want to come in? Pru went up to say goodnight, but I'm sure she and Marcel will be down soon."

My eyes went to the purse hanging from her shoulder. "You were leaving?"

A gentle smile. "It's getting late, and I figured I'd have a sexy hockey player showing up at my place soon." She patted her rounded belly. "Plus, I'm on an Oreo high, which pretty soon will be trailed by an Oreo crash, so I need to head home."

"And you want to give Pru and Marcel space," I presumed.

She froze and then her expression gentled. "Yeah," she whispered. "Even though they didn't know why I'd…" A shrug. "Well, they don't have the full story, and even though I talked to both of them, I knew they were worried. Pru got home late last night, and I gave them the day with Mila, but they needed face time, so when they invited me for dinner, I came."

I knew most of the timeline.

Had been there when Pru had called that morning, and Beth had told me during her text updates.

It was why I'd gotten Smitty to drop me here, even though we'd agreed to meet up later once she got home. I didn't even care that I'd be hearing about it in the locker room.

"You're a good friend," I whispered.

She gave another one of those nonplussed shrugs. "She'd be there for me."

Good friend.

Good woman.

"Yeah, she would," I agreed.

Laughter rang down the stairs—masculine and feminine and youthful—and Beth's face softened. "That's a good sound," she whispered.

It was.

From what Marcel had told me and the guys, Mila hadn't had much to laugh about.

Pru would light the way, Marcel would provide soft and gentle guidance, and both would give loyalty and love until their last breaths.

She hitched up her purse, shifted slightly from side to side.

"We should go," I offered.

Her eyes hit mine again. "You don't want—"

"I'll catch up with them later."

She blinked. "What?"

"Got it in you to give an annoying hockey player a ride home?"

Another blink. "What?" she asked again.

"Smitty gave me a ride over"—I slanted a glance at her car, parked at the curb—"think I can hitch a ride home?"

"Smitty?"

Right.

Too many details.

I shuffled her forward, out onto the porch, and reached for the door, closing it, and hitting the button on the bottom of the electronic keypad that would engage the dead bolt.

Then I shuffled her forward, down the steps, and to her car.

Her purse off her arm.

Keys out and locks bleeped.

"Get in, sugarpie."

The next blink had her face clearing. "Let me guess," she muttered. "You're driving me home?"

"*Us* home."

She gave me some tart. Just a dash of it, and I liked it. "I don't remember inviting you back to my place."

I grinned. "I invited myself."

"You were serious when you said *annoying* hockey player." A grumble that had amusement coiling through me.

I let it out, chuckling as I opened the passenger's side door. "I'm honest to a fault."

A sigh, but she folded herself into the seat. "You're lucky I'm on my Oreo crash and feeling too lazy to argue with you."

"Lucky," I agreed, grabbing, and dragging her seat belt across her.

"I can do that," she said, reaching for it.

Fingers on hers, stalling her movements. "I know you can."

I clicked the snap in place.

"Raph."

I ran my fingers along her jaw. "Humor me."

"I—" A spark in her eyes, but one she extinguished between one blink and the next. "Consider yourself humored." A beat. "This *one* time."

I laughed, straightened, and closed her door, rounding the hood and cramming himself into the driver's seat. She giggled as I folded himself in, fumbled to adjust the seat. "I know you're small," I teased, "but this is ridiculous."

"I'm not the one going all macho and having to drive."

"Considering I think my knees were up to my ears, I think I'll table the macho for the foreseeable future."

Another giggle. "Right," she said disbelievingly.

She got it.

Got *me*.

But not totally, because halfway through the ride she whispered, "You don't have to do this, you know."

"Do what?"

Her eyes were focused on the darkness out the window. "I'm probably not the smartest choice, considering all you went through."

My fingers tightened on the steering wheel. "I don't really think it's a choice."

She winced. I saw it in the reflection of the window, and reached for her, squeezing her leg lightly. "Don't tell me you don't feel it, too."

She turned, and I caught a glimpse of her face before I had to focus on the road.

It told me that she felt the same way as me.

"Exactly," I whispered. "This was going to happen. Always."

Silence.

"Yeah?" I asked.

"Yeah," she murmured after a moment.

"Sugarpie," I said as I drove carefully. "I need you to know that I've got my head together now. Part of that is because of you. Part of that is because I've realized that what really fucked me up was that I trusted my instincts about Monica. I thought she was a completely different person. I thought we were different together. And when she showed me different..."

Her hand hit my thigh, and she got what had been happening in my head faster than I had.

A hell of a lot faster.

"You lost trust in yourself," she whispered.

"Yeah, honey." I covered her hand with my own, squeezed.

She fell quiet.

I let her have that.

But as we closed in on her house, I gave her the rest. "I'm working on that, and my shit is sorted."

"And mine isn't," she whispered.

"Let me rephrase that," I said. "My shit is sorted for the *moment*. I'm sure we'll come to a point where it isn't, and where I'll need you to help me sort it."

Her chest expanded. Fell.

"Am I wrong?" I asked.

Quiet then, "No."

"So," I said, squeezing her hand, "what you need to know is that you helped me pull my head out of my ass after a year." I checked over my shoulder for traffic, changed lanes. "Then you had a moment and now you need *me* to be the steady. That's okay. That's life. That's how relationships work."

"But we haven't even been on a date."

My lips curved. "Is this you asking me out?"

"I—*Raph*—I'm being serious. I think you're a good guy and I like you a lot, but this"—she waved a hand at her head, her belly—"is a lot to deal with."

"I don't need easy and fake, Beth. I *need* a woman who's real."

"Raph," she whispered.

"I'm serious. I need a woman who can deal with real shit."

She turned to me, brows lifted, as though to say that her breakdown meant that she couldn't handle real shit.

Meanwhile, it showed me that she was a survivor, that she'd overcome and fought for the good things in her life.

"Fuck that," I said fiercely. "What you went through was not you being weak or not being able to deal—"

"I think having a panic attack and needing to be sedated in the hospital is the very definition of *not being able to deal*," she said, giving voice to those thoughts I'd seen in her eyes.

"That's bullshit."

"I—"

"It's *bullshit*, sugarpie." I squeezed her hand again. "You don't have to be perfect. You're allowed to have moments where you're not strong."

She went still.

Really still.

"Beth," I murmured when she didn't reply.

Her eyes, when they came to mine, were stark.

"Look, honey. I don't know what you've gone through. Though," I added quickly when shadows crossed her face, "I'm here to listen when you're ready to talk about it, whenever that might be."

Her inhale was sharp, her exhale was long and loud.

"But I do know that it's serious enough to have wounded you deeply. So deeply that you have panic attacks and night-mares—and this isn't me trying to get you to divulge everything here and now before you're ready. This is me respecting that you've been through things that hurt you, that affect you today, that make you *human*."

"I—" She clamped her teeth together.

"I also know that you may think you need to be perfect and steady and totally unaffected by everything from your past while you play superwoman and take care of everyone else." I laced our fingers together. "But you don't need to be that with me."

Her gaze went to the window. "We'd be better off ending this now."

"You don't need to be that with *me*, honey."

Her shoulders inched up. "You'd be *better* off."

"You don't need to be that with me," I repeated.

"This is me trying to take care of you," she said softly.

"I know."

"So you agree that we're not going further?"

"No," I said. "We're not giving up. We're not searching for perfect. We're going to be us and real and figure out if we want to keep being real together."

I'd meant the words to be a comfort, but they only seemed to make her shoulders inch up more.

"Beth."

Finally, she looked at me.

"We haven't even been on a first date, sugarpie."

Her expression was blank.

"At least give me that. One date. A real one, and then you can dump my ass if you want."

TWENTY-FOUR

Beth

I WAS DETERMINED to let him go.

Determined that what was best for him was not hanging around me and my mess, but since he'd clearly done some self-reflection and was moving in the right direction, he didn't need me to fix him.

He'd fixed himself.

So, I should let him go.

Because I definitely couldn't be *real* with him.

But he was staring at me with gorgeous blue eyes and talking to me with a soft voice and his expression was earnest and...

I'd wanted him for so long.

And...it was just one date.

"Shopping and water bottles didn't count as a date?" I asked lightly, trying to contain the hope and joy beginning to bubble in my heart.

"No, sugarpie."

"But we even had pretzels."

His gaze had returned to the road, but I saw the side of his mouth closest to me tip up.

And God, making him smile was...a fucking gift sent from above. It made everything inside me warm and thaw and not even *think* about that basement I'd filled with concrete.

"I see I got my work cut out for me," he said softly.

That sliced deep, and I couldn't stop myself from inhaling sharply.

Which he noticed.

I *knew* he did.

Because he seemed to notice everything.

But he didn't comment on it, didn't harp on it and demand answers. He just...let me have that, and I wasn't sure if I was disappointed or relieved or some strange combination of both.

"One date, sugarpie?" he pressed. "Just dinner and a movie or something equally as innocuous?"

There went that same combination of both disappointment and relief again.

He was Raph. He wasn't innocuous. He was...something bigger.

I wanted something bigger with him.

Which was probably why I stopped fighting it, decided that he'd been giving plenty, and just said, "Yes."

———

RAPH DROVE himself to his house and, no surprise since it seemed impossible for me to deny him anything, he'd tempted me inside for a tour.

One smile, a gentle question, and suddenly he'd been pulling my car into an empty spot in his garage, and I was walking into his kitchen.

Which was absolutely gorgeous.

Top-of-the-line appliances, loads of cabinets, a huge island with a slab of striking granite.

Now, I had a trust fund and plenty of money to buy my home, but his was nicer.

Bar none.

I caught a glimpse of a pool and hot tub in the back yard, lush greenery surrounding the pavers and making the pretty blue tile dipping into the top of the water really pop.

"That's all Lexi's doing," he murmured, catching sight of my gaze.

The GM's wife had a collection of green thumbs...and okay, that didn't sound right. I just meant that Lexi was really good with plants, loved landscaping as a hobby, and she'd advised more than a few of the men and women close to the Breakers on their yards. But then I wasn't thinking about plants.

I was thinking about *Raph*.

Mostly because he came close and dropped a hand on either side of me, resting them on the counter near my hips and making my breath catch.

Because he was close and big and yummy and smelled good and—

"Beth?"

"Mmm?"

"You good?"

I blinked. "I'm good. So Lexi picked out plants for you?"

Raph tucked a strand of hair behind my ear, smiled. "She straightened out my landscaper when I moved in. Got him sorted with the right plants for the climate and still texts him when it's time to fertilize or move the plants to different pots."

I laughed.

That sounded like Lexi.

She wasn't just the GM's wife and lawyer for the team, she was also well-known for her yearly gardening challenges with the team.

They involved her hubby's big, bad hockey players keeping a plant alive for the season.

The most successful one received a prize.

Which was considered a prize only in the loosest sense of the word. The winner—chosen by Lexi, who looked at each of the plants' growth and health (and truthfully, for some, that meant sadly dumping the pot's contents into the compost bin)— received a Fuggler.

Some combination of cute and ugly—but mostly ugly—it was fuzzy blue, wore tighty whities, and had maniacal eyes and life-sized plastic human teeth.

I'd seen it on Marcel's shelf one time, and that was enough to imprint the frightening image on my mind.

Forever.

"How do you do in the plant competitions?"

He nodded to the corner of his counter...and I laughed at the stringy and slightly dry-looking flower shoved to the side.

"Not a winner this year."

Thank God I wouldn't be coming across Mac, the Fuggler, in his house.

"Wasn't feeling like doing much except focusing on the bad shit and making myself feel miserable."

And shit, now I felt guilty.

I stilled. "Raph," I murmured.

His fingers drifted across my cheek. "Took me a while to stop feeling sorry for myself."

"Monica was—"

"It wasn't her, honey. Like I said, or not *all* her anyway. It was me, too. Losing faith in myself, hating that I hadn't seen her for what she was."

My heart squeezed tight. "Raph," I whispered again. "I think it's normal to feel that way. It was a big lie and the death of a future you'd imagined."

"Yeah." A breath then a deliberate change in subject. "Want to see the rest of the house?"

He'd given me space in the car. He'd noticed that my pain lay deeper than what I wanted to share, but he hadn't pushed, hadn't prodded at the weak spot. He'd given me space, allowed me to regroup.

So, I gave him that change, that space, that time to regroup and come to terms.

"Yeah," I whispered. "I do."

A step back, his hand taking mine.

And then he led me into a large great room with cozy furniture, a huge TV, and shelves filled with gaming systems. I'd been around enough, had spent enough time at Oliver and Hazel's and Marcel and Pru's places to see how the boys could be with their video games (hell, they'd nearly had a brawl during a round-robin *Fruit Ninja* competition one night over pizza, beer, and margaritas), so Raph having a full setup didn't surprise me either.

It did make me smile, just like the furniture—nice and expensive, but not fancy, definitely sturdy enough to hold a bevy of hockey players—made my heart warm.

This was a home.

A place for friends and family to be at *home*.

He led me on, through bathrooms that were the height of luxury, a master bedroom twice the size of mine, a huge gym with a treadmill, a Peloton, and lots of free weights. He walked me through an office with full bookshelves and bright windows and a big desk that I could imagine Raph sitting behind.

All of it was beautiful and positively sumptuous.

But it wasn't stuffy.

It was comfortable.

And...as he led me back down the hall toward the staircase, I saw there was a door closed in the hall.

Raph noticed my hesitation.

And I watched him battle, expecting him to lead me on, back downstairs, back into the kitchen and the garage and to my car so that I could drive home.

But then he used his free hand to grip the knob, to turn it.

And...my heart squeezed tight, so tight that I actually went dizzy for a moment. But just a moment because then I was able to pull myself together and study the nursery as he flicked on the lights.

Wide wooden letters spelling the name Luca.

Fuck.

"I haven't been in here, not since I found out," he said softly.

"Luca is a beautiful name," I whispered.

"My grandfather's name."

Fuck, I wished again that I could kill that bitch.

"It's beautiful."

He nodded, taking a step inside, as though proving to himself that he could, and when that was accomplished, he nodded again, just slightly.

Like he'd just ticked off an item on his to-do list.

Or maybe, he was just trying to survive doing something that was difficult, something that he hadn't been able to do up until that point.

Definitely that.

I squeezed his fingers, and he tore his gaze from the room—from the crib, bookcases, rocking chair, changing table, from the copious stuffed animals and blankets and clothes, the cozy rug —to me.

"Fancy a hot chocolate?"

I blinked.

"I make a mean hot cocoa," he said, sliding his fingers up my arm, coming close and tucking me under his shoulder. "Do you want one?"

His tone was soft, the pain in his eyes was dimmer than I'd ever seen, as if by opening that door and stepping inside had brought everything up, but that bringing hadn't flayed him open. Hadn't exposed him to all that hurt again. Grief still present, a grief that would always be there, I knew, because he'd lost a dream, future, a deeply woven hope. But it was tempered, as time often allowed, as looking forward to new dreams, new futures, new hopes did the same.

Another layer of concrete.

Looking forward not back, not down.

Looking into the beautiful blue eyes of a man I liked so, *so* much.

"Yes," I whispered. "I'd like that hot chocolate."

TWENTY-FIVE

Raph

IT WAS 5:59 P.M., and I was walking up the steps that led to Beth's front door.

She'd stayed at my place last night.

Not necessarily her idea, but because I'd plied her with two mugs of my special hot chocolate (which wasn't really special hot chocolate at all, just expensive chocolate, a dollop of caramel, and a large pinch of cumin).

My mother's recipe.

Though I never could be bothered to whip my own cream.

She was gone now, too.

Had left me when I was thirteen, in the hands of my father.

Another disappointment, or two, rather—the leaving of my mother, the resultant anger and abuse from my sperm donor of a father.

Thank God for hockey.

And, truthfully, thank God for my big ass hockey body. I'd gotten big early in life, lived up to the giant hockey player stereotype. I was no Smitty, but I was six-three, two hundred pounds. I'd gotten taller than my father early, had bulked up because time in the gym meant time away from home when my mother had left.

That bulk had been slimmed as years went on, as I focused on speed and flexibility.

But I was still big, much bigger than Beth.

And much bigger than my sperm donor, who'd lost interest when he realized he couldn't bully me.

"Raph?"

I blinked, realized I'd been standing there on Beth's porch like an idiot, back in the past, in my head, thinking about shit that I'd wanted to long forget, and...running late, I thought, cursing softly as I glanced down at my watch.

This was my last free evening for more than a week, what with the season heating up and a road trip on the calendar, and I was standing, staring at nothing, thinking about long-dead shit, wasting time when I didn't have a whole lot of it, especially this time of year.

"Hey, sugarpie," I murmured, bending and sliding my lips across hers.

Her tongue dipped out and the brush of mouths turned deeper.

"I missed you," she whispered.

My hot chocolates had made her drowsy, and paired with fresh popcorn and an action movie, she'd fallen asleep in my arms. I'd taken advantage, not moving her, not so much as twitching a muscle for fear of waking her.

Not until the movie was over and my own eyelids were growing heavy.

Then I'd shifted her against my chest, carried her up the stairs and into my bedroom, holding tight to my control so I didn't kiss her, wake her up, and taste every inch of her again.

I needed to be smart now. To move slowly.

To not trigger her fear and panic again.

I cupped Beth's cheek. "You just miss my hot chocolate."

"Nope." A grin. "It was the popcorn. That seasoning on top." She chef kissed.

I grinned, slid her close, tucked her under my shoulder, where she fit perfectly, where I could feel her, soak in her warmth, scent the soft floral perfume of her hair sprayed across her skin. The seasoning I'd sprinkled over the top of the popcorn was another one of my mother's specialties—mostly salt, but also a dash of pepper, a teaspoon of sugar, and a pinch of cinnamon all mixed in with the buttery, oily goodness.

It was delicious.

But then again, most of my mother's cooking had been.

It had been most of the good she'd left me, and the memories were the rest. Because what came after—

A hand on my jaw, and I glanced down into Beth's concerned face. "What is it?" she asked.

I didn't want to talk about this. I wanted to concentrate on the now, on this date with Beth. I didn't want to drag up the past.

But how could I expect that she would share hers if I continued to bury mine deep?

It was why I'd opened the door the night before.

It was time for me to let the wounds in me air out, to heal in the light, to allow the shadows I'd carried for too long to be extinguished.

So I said, "My parents weren't great. Dad was—*is*—an asshole who likes to drink too much, yell too much, smoke too much, and work too little. Mom got tired of it. Left me. Left me, and I didn't hear from her until after we won our first Cup. She wanted me to bring it to her so her kids from the new family she'd created could see it."

Silence.

Then, Beth's voice shook with anger. "Are you serious?"

A quiet question, but the words reverberated through me.

"Unfortunately, yes."

A breath, her eyes snapping and sparking, as though she were an avenging angel.

"It's a shitty truth, sugarpie, but it is my truth." A shrug. Not to dismiss it, but because my shoulders were taut and I needed to loosen the tension. "I had a lot of shit—parents, teachers, coaches—but I've shoveled my way out of it now," I said. "I've got good friends now. A good woman." I smoothed my thumb along her bottom lip. "And a good family that I've created. We're not related, but I don't need biology to tell me what is a good thing and what's not."

Her lips parted.

"For the record, *you're* a good thing. *You're* the good woman."

Dampness drifting across blue eyes.

"And you're part of that good family I've been lucky enough to create."

Her shoulders lifted, pushing against the underside of my arm. Then dropped. "Raph," she whispered, the tip of her tongue dipping out, dampening her lips, tempting me again, wanting to taste and take.

"I'm okay, honey."

"They shouldn't be like that."

"No," I whispered. "They shouldn't. But they are, and there's no changing it, no going back."

Her mouth pressed flat.

Then she sighed again.

Her mouth relaxed. "I hate that you had that."

"Me too. But"—my fingers on her cheek—"it also showed me what kind of man, what kind of parent I won't ever be."

Something stark in her eyes, her face.

Her body going so *so* still.

Fuck.

But almost as quickly, the stillness eased. "How are you so fucking gorgeous inside and out?" she whispered, her fingers sliding over my jaw, over the bristles already growing there, even though I'd shaved just before I'd left the house.

"Most beautiful woman I've ever seen," I whispered back.

Her cheeks went a little pink, but she didn't argue with me, just joked lightly, "Well, aren't we all about the compliments?"

I laughed softly. "Misery loves company?"

"If misery is me being with a man who calls me beautiful, then I can't really complain now, can I?"

"No," I said on a grin. "I don't think you can."

Her arm came around my waist. "Then I think we should prolong our misery, don't you?"

I loved that she was joking.

I loved that she was smiling with me and cuddling close.

I loved that we'd just created our first inside joke.

I loved...her.

That truth didn't course through me like a shock, didn't lock my muscles, make my breath catch. It merely settled onto my soul like a feather drifting down to the ground, slowly wobbling until it rested gently on the soil below.

That was it exactly.

A settling.

I loved her.

Yes, that was right.

"More misery," I said, shuffling her forward so she could lock her door and then guiding her to my car. "Consider it coming right up."

TWENTY-SIX

Beth

HE'D SAID he was going to take me to a movie and to dinner.

Something innocuous.

Something simple and low pressure.

This was...

A freaking helicopter.

"What are you doing?" I whispered when he parked at the airfield.

"We're going to dinner." He said it casually. Like we hadn't just parked next to a sleek-looking helicopter. "I'll have to rain check you on the movie, though, so I hope you'll give me a chance for a second date."

"What are you doing?" I whispered again.

"I have reservations at Lokanta."

My eyes widened, heart beginning to thud against my ribs. "What are you doing?" I whispered a third time.

He unbuckled his seat belt, turned to face me, unclicking my restraint, catching it so that it didn't whip back, drawing it slowly across my body until it was fully retracted. Then his fingers were on my jaw. "Dinner, sugarpie." He smiled, and it held just a bit of mischief. "Plus, I had some inside info and know it's your favorite restaurant."

It was.

It was one of the few things I missed from New York City.

Delicious Thai food. Staff that knew my name from my frequent dine-in and take-out trips and always had a ready smile for me. A quiet street tucked in the corner of a busy city center. One of *my* places in a life I'd tried to create on my own.

I'd taken Pru and Hazel there when they visited.

Of course, I had.

But I hadn't expected them to have understood how important it was to me.

God, I loved them.

God, I loved this *man*. Loved that he'd cared enough to ask. Loved that he was kind and thoughtful and a good friend. Loved his body and mind and heart. Loved *him*.

The concrete rumbled. The demons rattled at their doors.

And for the first time ever I didn't just wish the demons would vacate the castle, would cease to exist...I also wished that I could tell someone about them, could somehow do something to negate their power over me.

What would it be like to live without those demons?

Hazel would help me with that.

She *had* helped me with it, had connected me with Marin.

And that card was in my purse, my wallet.

And...I hadn't so much as called the number.

Because I was—

No. I wouldn't go down that path. Not tonight. Not again. Not fucking *ever*. I slapped another layer of concrete down, threw an iron door into the walkway that led down to the basement.

I turned to Raph. "What if I said I was afraid of flying?" I asked softly.

His face went blank. No, not *blank*. It went careful, as though he were studying me, trying to sort out if there was a wrong answer. But then it seemed to change, going back to just Raph. Gentle still, but also with warm blue eyes and a soft jaw. "Then we would do something else."

"Just like that?"

Quiet again, studying me. "Just like that, sugarpie."

"I—" I broke off, heart pounding, and it was ridiculously hard to admit, "Not used to that, Raph."

A beat. Then a soft, "I know."

Heart still pounding, but the words came slightly easier now. "Didn't see that growing up either." What my father said went. What my stepfather decreed had to be obeyed, for risk of—

"I didn't either."

I stared into gorgeous blue eyes; knew he wasn't humoring me.

At the beginning of this, I'd wanted to fix him, to make him smile and feel again and do all that feeling while being happy. But he was jackhammering at my defenses, at the concrete, and he was making me feel so much, *too* much, but...

It was addicting.

It was impossible to resist.

It was—for all my talk of healing him and then moving on— it was something I wasn't willing to give up. Not yet.

And maybe...if I talked to Marin, if I fixed the cracks, maybe I could banish the demons, and maybe I could keep Raph.

That had my heart pounding even harder.

That had hope curling through my middle.

I reached over and touched his jaw. My heart didn't slow. If anything, my pulse picked up the pace, and I suggested, "Maybe we can make something different from what we both had?"

Eyes as warm as the Caribbean, hot white sand beneath my toes, a sticky, humid breeze over my skin. "Yeah, honey. I'd like that."

Love.

Hope.

A man whose smile was as beautiful as it was gentle.

The demons didn't have a chance.

"BETH!" Achara exclaimed. "It's so good to see you, young lady —" She been reaching for my hands, but then her eyes widened, no doubt catching my new belly.

Rounded enough that I wasn't just looking like I'd participated in consuming too many tacos, but that I was actually pregnant...and since I was pregnant with twins, my belly was definitely noticeable.

Even more so since I was wearing one of my old wrap dresses and it was skintight and—

Belly time.

For sure.

Achara's hands squeezed mine. "Congratulations," she whispered.

"I—" I started to explain that they weren't my babies, same as I always did when someone asked about the pregnancy, but Achara's gaze went over my shoulder.

"Oh, is this your young man?"

That had me smiling, Raph and I were maybe a sum total of five years younger than Archara, but she called everyone young lady or man.

"This is Raph," I said softly.

"Her man," Raph agreed. "Though the jury is still out on whether or not I'm young."

Achara smiled, glanced back down at me, mouthing, "He's cute."

I mouthed back, "Yeah. He is."

That smile widened. "If you want a table, I can squeeze you guys in, but it might be a bit of a wait."

"I actually made a reservation. Raphael Gomez at eight."

Achara was positively beaming now. "Oh, *you're* Raph," she said a bit mystically before she glanced down at the list in front of her, making a few notes and then nodding behind her. "If you'll follow me."

No picking up menus.

No further explanations or questions.

Just that cryptic smile and Achara leading us to a booth in a quiet corner of the restaurant, Raph's thigh pressed to mine, his body warm, and the spicy male scent of him surrounding me.

Then, with a squeeze to my shoulder, she was gone.

Before I could ask about menus—not that *I* needed them. I was boring and always ordered the same thing, but Raph would probably want a look. And anyway, it never hurt to look. Maybe this would be the one time that I would change things up.

Nah.

Who was I kidding?

That wasn't going to happen.

I was going to get *Tom Yum Goong, Som Tum,* and then because I could never decide between them, both *Tom Kha Kai* and *Gaeng Daeng*—spicy shrimp soup and spicy green papaya salad and chicken in coconut soup *and* red curry.

Hey. I was eating for three.

(Never mind that I'd ordered the same, even not pregnant).

"Do you want—"

Our server appeared, carrying two glasses, which she plunked down on the table, and before I could ask for those menus, she was gone again.

"I—"

A warm hand on my nape. "Relax, sugarpie. Food is coming—unless you want to step out of your usual?" He paused, and I shook my head, causing his expression to soften. "Then just breathe and enjoy being here."

"You arranged it all." Not a question, or not really phrased as one. But still one anyway.

"It's our first date," he said. Not an answer. But still one anyway.

My heart squeezed. "Raph," I whispered.

He didn't let us get drawn back into the past or my fears or what we'd both missed out on. Instead, he just lifted a glass, placed it in my hand, and then he lifted his, clinking it to mine. "To a beautiful woman, and a future that will be happy and whole."

I sipped—and no surprise—it was my favorite iced tea, perfectly sweetened.

Another crack in the cement.

But instead of demons escaping, there was just happiness... and hope.

Hope that blossomed when all my favorites were delivered to the table in turn. Hope that grew even bigger when instead of dessert from Lokanta—which was delicious like all their food but wasn't my favorite—Achara delivered a box of passionfruit and whipped cream-filled cream puffs from her bakery just a couple of blocks over. *Those* were my favorites.

Those had me turning to Raph and sliding my arms around his shoulders, hugging him tight and whispering into his ear, "I really like you."

His husky reply, "I more than really like you, sugarpie."

Then he kissed me.

And if I hadn't already been in love with Raph, that kiss, the hope that filled me from toes to top, would have.

Or maybe the way he promptly opened the box and served me up a cream puff would have.

Or maybe the way he held my hand as we exited the restaurant, blocking anyone coming close to bumping into me in the crowded space, tucking me close as we walked back down the sidewalk and to the car would have.

But I was already in deep, and I knew that I wouldn't be able to let him go, not after this.

I was in for the long haul, in for the man, even if it meant that business card and Marin and facing those demons.

Because I had Raph and his gentle eyes, his soft smiles, that laughter, and the kisses, and his body protecting mine.

Because I had love and hope in my heart.

If only...

If only that hope had lasted.

TWENTY-SEVEN

Raph

HER HAND HADN'T LEFT mine since she'd finished with her cream puffs.

They were delicious—the two that I'd allowed myself to eat, considering it was the middle of the season and I'd already eaten my body weight, it seemed, in delicious Thai food. Plus, they were hers. I'd arranged for her to have them, so they were for her.

But next time I was in the city for a game, I was picking some up for myself and the guys.

Maybe some I'd have filled with that passion fruit cream.

Maybe I'd fill a couple with other things—mustard, maybe, relish...apparently, I could only think of sandwich condiments. But it'd be a good way to get Smitty back for being a pain in the ass...and it would get me back to my old tricks.

Or pranks.

Plus, I'd get another chance to bring Beth a treat that had

started her smiling and kept her smiling the entire helicopter flight home.

Or maybe that was just this night.

It was magical...and not just the time we'd spent together. It was more, as though I'd gotten behind her walls. She'd given. She'd *talked* to me, not putting me off or closing down. But she'd actually talked about her life in New York before she'd moved to Baltimore—her favorite places, her job, the things she'd liked to do, her regular haunts. Not just trying to make me laugh or talk about myself. She'd shared.

So, I was riding my own high, feeling like I'd won the game to win all games.

Except, it was more important than any game I'd ever played.

So, I was enjoying the moment, soaking in the gains I'd made, but I was also planning the next steps, how to gain momentum and not lose ground.

"Raph?"

I blinked, realized I'd been so lost in my head that I'd driven us back to my place, and shit, that wasn't what I'd been planning on doing. I was going to drive Beth home, coax a kiss out of her, and then leave her on her doorstep because I had to catch an early afternoon flight and it was late.

Instead, we were sitting inside my garage, the engine of my car still running even as the heavy metal door slid closed behind us.

"Just saying, if you're trying for murder, the proper time was before you shelled out for dinner, helicopter rides, and specialty cream puffs."

Funny.

Always making me smile.

"I meant to take you home," I said. "I didn't want—"

"I wanted," she said. "I *want*."

My breath caught...and truthfully, my dick went hard.

"And the bonus is that here is closer than my place."

"I have to fly out tomorrow."

"I know," she said. "So, I'll catch a Lyft in the morning." Her fingers flexed slightly. "Or you can drop me at home."

"Or," I whispered, aware that I could be pushing too much too fast, "you could just stay and hang here and borrow my car if you need to get home."

"Your car?"

"Smitty and I carpool."

That was a lie, and my friend would give me no little amount of shit for it. But if it meant that Beth would stay, would sleep in my bed, would make a small place for herself in my home...

Yeah, I'd gladly shovel it.

Gladly.

"How about I stay tonight?" she said softly. "And tomorrow we'll play it by ear."

That sounded...far better than anything I could have hoped for.

"Works for me," I murmured, hitting the button to turn off my car and then getting out, rounding the hood.

Beth's slender ankles were just visible beneath the gap at the bottom of the door as she unbuckled and stepped out of her side. In flats, because she was Beth and carrying Pru and Marcel's precious cargo, so of course she was. But they were no less sexy, and neither was the dress, showing her curves, showing her belly, a belly that didn't bring a twinge of pain any longer.

I'd come to understand it for exactly what it was.

Love.

Beth's love.

So, it brought me pride and respect and *love.*

Beth took my hand as she moved around the door, and I drew her close and inhaled deeply. "Love the way you smell, sugarpie."

She smiled, tapped her nose. "You do pretty good yourself. And that's coming from this bloodhound of a nose. I feel like I can be a master perfumer."

I tucked a lock of her hair behind her ear. "I heard that can happen during pregnancy."

"Lucky"—she pressed closer, and my cock twitched at the contact—"my body likes the way you smell."

My body liked hers. Period. The way she smelled, how she felt, every single inch of her. It liked her a whole fucking lot.

But...

Slow.

Causing no panic. No pain. No unwelcome dredging of the past.

I just wanted us to build a foundation so that when she was comfortable, she could come to me, share that past when she was ready.

Didn't mean my dick wasn't hard for her though.

Didn't mean my dick didn't throb when she pressed herself to me.

But instead of lowering my head and kissing her like I wanted to, I started to back away, to lead her into the house and to bed.

It was a late night.

She was growing two babies.

She needed her rest.

"You know," she murmured, when I'd flicked on the kitchen lights and started to draw her through the space, "I've been thinking about these counters."

That had me frowning, not following. "Okaaay," I began.

"And I've been thinking about my dress."

I had too.

Been thinking many, *many* things, but mostly about how it would look when it was crumpled into a pile on the floor.

"Yeah," I agreed, and no lie, my voice ended up a rasp as she slipped her hand free, trailing the fingers that had been laced with mine just moments before across the counter. I wanted them drifting across my chest, lower, dipping down beneath the waistband of my pants, wrapping around my cock, stroking hard and fast and—

"I've been thinking about how my dress was made."

That I hadn't been thinking about.

That I wouldn't *ever* think about.

On sexy. Off better.

"I was thinking about how if I pull this"—my gaze jerked to her, watched her hand drift toward her middle—"then my entire dress will come loose."

Wait, what?

But then her fingers, nails painted a bright red to match her lipstick, were moving again, drifting along the bodice of her dress, closing around a thin strip of fabric, and tugging.

Holy shit.

It was like a fucking magic trick.

One second my woman was fully clothed.

The next, the material was open, sliding down her arms, puddling to the floor, and looking damned good there. But that held my focus for only a heartbeat because Beth was there, and while she wasn't naked, the little clothing she *was* wearing did nothing to cover her and absolutely everything to enhance, to tease, to tempt.

Black lace that cut so low her nipples seemed as though they would pop free with just one deep breath. Fire engine red ribbons attached to black mesh stockings. Panties that were barely there and—

She turned around.

Sweet Christ.

Her underwear had a tiny red bow just at the precipice of both cheeks.

"So, I was thinking"—she spun back to face me, and fucking hell, those nipples *did* pop free, not with a deep breath, though, but rather, with an arch of her back—"that last time didn't go so well, so maybe we can try a different position."

My cock twitched, and I tried to stop to think.

But I barely had any blood left in my brain and the gears of my mind were working really slow.

Slow. *Slow.*

Right. I was supposed to be slowing things down.

Like a first date via a helicopter and taking her to my house was slow.

Not the point.

"Honey," I whispered. "I think we'd better take things slow."

Silence.

Then, "Do you *want* to take them slow? Is this too much?"

Concern in her eyes and voice and none of the liquid desire from a moment before. Fuck. "This isn't too much," I said, stepping close, even as I tried to keep my hands to myself. "But I don't know what happened last time, sugarpie. I don't want to do something that might trigger—"

"It wasn't you."

I blinked.

"I was thinking about everything in my past and how that moment was so good. And I started spiraling, knowing that it couldn't last, that something would ruin it"—a breath that brushed her breasts across my chest—"that *I* would ruin it," she whispered. "Because I always ruin the good things in my life."

"Baby—"

"I'm starting to realize that was shit implanted by my step-dad, because of what happened to my mom."

I held my breath.

"I thought I could bury it." A beat. "I thought I *should* bury it. But…" Her lips turned up into a sad smile. "I'm finally starting to think that's a bad habit."

I slid my hands down her arms. "I'm glad."

"Now." She exhaled, started to reach for her dress. "I know I killed the mood, so we should just call it a night and—"

I halted her with a hand on her chin. "Freeze."

Now she inhaled. "What?"

I trailed a finger over her collarbone, dipped it down and used it to circle her nipple. "I have this perfectly good countertop and my woman just performed a fucking spectacular magic trick a couple of minutes ago."

That breath slid out.

"See," I murmured, dropping my head, and trailing my mouth along her throat. "I have this fantasy, and it involves a counter and my woman naked and—"

She reached between us, pushed up slightly on my jaw, lifting my head. "*You* see," she began. "*I* have this fantasy and it involves a countertop and me naked and my man thrusting into me hard and deep and fast."

Blood boiled.

My cock got harder.

Slow disappeared.

Hard and deep and fast took over.

And…it turned out that both of our fantasies were the same.

Beth

I WAS SITTING in Raph's bed, having somehow been convinced to sleep there that night, even though he wasn't going to be home.

Convinced even after we'd gone back to my place for a change of clothes and my laptop so I could work. Convinced even though I hadn't put on those clothes, hadn't bothered for once to put on my makeup.

Because I didn't need the shield.

Because he wasn't my father.

Because...I'd had another nightmare last night, another dream twisted with a memory of my stepfather beating my mother. I'd woken up on a start, but Raph was already there, grounding me in the present, hands gentle on my body, voice soft.

And I'd told him what had happened.

Too many times to count.

I'd told him how I'd hidden and whispered about the *thunks* that I hadn't understood were my stepfather's fists.

I'd told him how my father was strict and stern, but never got physical as far as I was aware. Though, I had been young when he'd died, so there was a possibility my mother had picked poorly twice.

The first time, a man who had nearly bankrupted our family, and if not for the money from my mother's family, then we would have lost our house—and no six-year-old should be privy to that kind of information, should worry about having to sell my toys to find a way to keep it. Luckily, we'd been bailed out by my mother's family and then because my father had died, the excess spending had been halted.

Our house had been safe.

My mother and I had been happy.

But only for a short time.

Because then my stepfather had entered the picture.

Rich in his own right, he brought no risk of losing our home —in fact, he still lived in the house I'd grown up in.

But he was so much worse.

Because my stepfather had been strict and stern *and* added abusive to the mix. *That* was what I'd been dreaming of.

No.

That was what my recurring nightmares were about.

How I could still hear, still *feel* those noises.

Still see myself in the corner of my room.

Could still remember the fear gripping me as I moved down the hall.

Could still feel the pain as his fists collided with my little body, hurting *so much* when I'd tried to intervene, tried to protect my mother. He'd never picked spots that would show, not for either of us, but he'd picked locations that would *hurt*.

Bad.

So badly that at some point...I'd stopped trying to intervene.

At some point, I'd stayed hidden and tried to ignore the noises, tried to pretend they weren't happening.

And I'd told Raph all of that before the sun had come up, when he should have been resting for his game, after waking him up in the middle of the night, and...he wasn't upset with me.

He'd listened.

He'd held me.

And...he hadn't judged me.

I'd watched his face closely, not letting my gaze so much as slide away. Not hiding because I needed to watch for a change, to see if this glimpse into my past, into *me*, would have him looking at me differently.

But his expression didn't change.

No disgust, no loathing or revulsion. He'd just been himself in that moment—soft and gentle...and God, I loved him.

And just that easy...several of my demons had been vanquished.

There were more.

Bigger ones, uglier ones.

But I couldn't deny that some part of myself was testing him, giving him something heavy and dark and seeing how he dealt.

Maybe that wasn't right.

But he'd passed my test, and the stranglehold on my insides, the pounding always present in the deepest recesses of my mind, had eased.

I'd been able to go back to sleep when I'd never been able to do that before.

Later, I'd woken to his lips on my brow, a plate of strawberry jellied toast on the nightstand.

Love.

Big and bold and filling every vein and capillary, every artery and cell.

So that was why I was in Raph's bed, in his T-shirt, not a stitch of makeup on my face—not even my lipstick, *gasp!*—and watching the Breakers play.

It meant something completely different, watching Raph out on the ice, knowing he was mine, knowing that I wasn't going to play the martyr, wasn't going to just cut and run, pretending it was best for him, when really, it was safer for myself.

To hide my past, keep my demons locked behind heavy wooden doors.

Because he might look at me...like how I felt when I stared at my reflection in the mirror, like how my family had looked at me when they found out the truth, like—

The babies in my belly rolled, jerking me out of my mind, placing me fiercely in the present.

And fuck, I was tired of spending so much time in the past.

I wanted more moments like last night, not worrying about demons and concrete and wooden doors.

I wanted more time with Raph.

But the demons weren't going to go away all on their own.

And I knew that I couldn't dump everything on Raph, every memory and complicated feeling. Just as I knew that I needed to share, I also understood that I needed to sort my shit if I wanted to have something good with Raph.

Which was why I was sitting on his bed, in his T-shirt, the blankets pulled up and over my legs, his pillows tucked behind my back. Tucked there by his hands. Thoughtful and kind hands that didn't hurt, same as they'd left the snacks on the nightstand, and same as they'd cupped my cheek, kissing me softly when he'd gone to catch the plane.

All of that.

I had all of that.

And I didn't want to lose it.

So, I was sitting on his bed, in his shirt, and holding Marin's card.

It was after hours, but I knew if I waited until the morning to call, I would find some excuse to continue avoiding facing this.

I needed to face it.

I needed to excise this.

I needed to finally, *finally* move on with my life.

Still, I'd avoided this for decades. It wasn't easy to shed that weight...so it took me until the second intermission to dial the number.

The sound of the first ring in my ear nearly sent my finger to the end button.

But I took a breath, held on, and listened to the second ring.

The third.

"Hello?"

Marin's voice coming through the speaker nearly had me dropping my cell, and it certainly had my lungs freezing, lips tightening, any words I might have spoken (I'd been mentally plotting the voicemail I was going to leave) being locked up in the back of my throat.

"Hello?" Marin asked again.

I opened my mouth, but nothing came up.

"*Hello?*" It was impatient this time, as though Marin was getting ready to hang up.

"Marin," I croaked.

The voice eased. "This is her."

Right. Marin had been on my mind a whole lot, but I was probably just another patient, albeit one that had been referred through a friend. Easily forgettable. Easily discounted—

Enough.

Shit, was this really the pattern I'd been on for fucking *years?*

It was.

And it was time to change.

"Marin," I said, straightening my shoulders, lifting my chin, glad that when my voice came out it was steady. "This is Beth, Hazel's friend." A breath. My heart pounding like I'd run a marathon, and I supposed I had, albeit a mental one. "I know you said you wouldn't get in my head, but...what if I open the gates and *let* you in?"

Right.

I was lined up.

The horn had just blown.

Now all I needed to do was put one foot in front of the other and start covering those miles.

Silence. Long enough that I practically saw myself tripping over my own feet, face-planting on the asphalt. Then Marin spoke. "You sure you're ready for that? I think you get that I don't beat around the bush, and if you're locked down tight..."

I sat in the quiet of Marin trailing off, taking a beat, considering, breathing, and...knowing.

Knowing that I was ready.

That I couldn't keep doing this.

That it was time.

"I'm ready," I whispered.

Marin didn't make me wait for it, didn't make me work any harder for it. Instead, she just said, "I have Tuesday at five open."

TWENTY-NINE

Raph

"YOU NEED TO GET A BETTER PICKER," Smitty said as we all got dressed after the game. We were in the away locker room at the arena, since we were on the road, and while our equipment and support staff did their best to give us everything we might need...

It wasn't home.

Or maybe it was just that Beth was in my bed, waiting for me to join her there.

It would be late, so I wouldn't wake her, but I was damn sure going to wake her as early as was reasonable...and if that ended up after I'd gotten just a couple of hours of sleep, then so be it.

I had a list of sexual fantasies to get through.

And I was finding that Beth was just as creative in bed as I was.

Meanwhile, though, I was trying to play it cool. Mostly because Smitty hadn't spilled the beans yet. Something I knew was coming because I'd asked Pru and Hazel for insider information and they'd only given it when they knew what the date was...and hell, who was I kidding? Everyone was being *real* cool, but my and Beth's time *not* being a conversation topic in the locker room would only last so long, and then all eyes would be on me and Beth and our relationship—

"My picker isn't broken," Cas protested.

Thankfully, Cas's inability to date a normal woman was still the hot subject matter up for discussion rather than me and my pursuit of Beth.

Theo snorted. "That's what you said about bringing that girl to CeCe's." He shook his head. "Now you and I have had to dodge her the last three times we visited."

"Carrie was an exception," Cas protested. "Normally my picker is on point."

Smitty began ticking off on his giant ass fingers. "Carrie. Margaret. Rosa. Becky. Lisa." A shrug. "And those are just the ones I remember from this season."

Cas yanked up his pants. "I'm not into commitment unless it's the right person."

"Which is just my point," Smitty said, sitting—still naked because the man would walk through life buck ass naked if he could and not get arrested—on the bench, rubbing his hair with a towel. "You need a better picker." A beat, his gaze dipping toward mine before heading back to Cas's. "To find the right person."

"Why are you up my ass about a picker—which is the dumbest thing I've ever said, by the way," Cas muttered.

"Definitely not the *dumbest*," Theo said with a smirk. "You forget that I've spent time around you when you're drunk."

Cas glared at Theo but didn't comment. "I'm not the only single fucker on this team. Just because you and Marcel are settled doesn't mean the rest of us—"

"One," Smitty boomed, "you've said multiple times you *want* to be settled like Marcel and me. Two, your *picker* sucks." A wave of his hand. "Hence my list from before."

"And *I'm* just saying that I'm not the only one who's single," Cas grumbled. "Theo is free and loose. Raph is probably ready to get back in the saddle. Bug him, or Walker, or—" He froze, probably because Smitty and Marcel had both deliberately glanced away from Cas and me *and* miracle of all miracles, Smitty began getting dressed (Marcel was just finishing buttoning his shirt) without adding further comment.

The avoidance gave me a whole new appreciation for Pru and Hazel and their relationships with their men. I also had to add Kailey—Smitty's other half—to the list, because the quiet woman, who occasionally hung with Pru, Hazel, and Beth (though she was closer to Oliver, Hazel's husband, since they bonded over nerdy things like spreadsheets and video games) was somehow keeping Smitty in check.

He'd clocked my interest.

He could be letting the gossip flow.

But Kailey was quiet, very quiet, and preferred to keep her business to herself.

So *that* and Hazel and Pru clearly getting how big a step last night was for me and Beth must have convinced their men to keep it under wraps.

I was going to buy them flowers.

Or maybe Hazel flowers and Pru that new hockey stick she was lusting after and Kailey, who I suspected had managed the biggest feat of all—getting Smitty to shut it—I was stocking her up with gift cards for her dragon game.

I watched Cas's brows pull together, probably mentally recounting what he'd just said that had Marcel and Smitty avoiding his gaze. "Walker?"

"Not interested in settling down," Walker chimed in, teeth

flashing as he ran his hand through his hair, leaving the locks in a haphazard arrangement that I had heard more than one female fan sigh over.

A beat as Cas processed that.

Then Cas's eyes found mine, surprise in the forest green depths. "Raph?"

Smitty—*somehow*—didn't say a word.

It was Theo that let the gossip loose, the fucker.

"It's Beth."

I glared at my teammate.

Cas blinked—once, twice, and then his mouth curved. "I *knew* it."

"Oh yeah, brother," Smitty said, seemingly deciding that since Theo had let the cat out of the bag that he was going to chime right in. "Totally perfect for him."

"Christ," I muttered, shoving my feet into my shoes. "Is this really what passes for locker room talk nowadays?"

"Fuck yeah, it is," Cas said, probably just relieved the attention had turned from him.

I sighed but didn't engage. That was the best-case scenario when it came to Smitty.

"You know it is," Marcel said quietly, though he was smiling widely, the fucker.

"I'm more interested in hearing who Smitty thinks Cas should date," Theo said.

That worked for me *and* it pulled my friend out of the dog house. Marginally, anyway, considering he'd spilled the beans in the first place.

Apparently Smitty talking about Cas and his picker was more interesting too—either that or he was afraid of fallout with Kailey—because he grabbed onto that conversational gambit, detailing who he, if he played matchmaker, would set Cas up with—a woman with a great laugh, a hard worker who was smart, and tall with great tits and a nice ass wouldn't go amiss.

I agreed with most of the list.

Tall wasn't necessary.

Beth was small and curvy, and that made for all sorts of interesting creativity to get our bodies to connect in all the *right* ways.

"Good list," Theo muttered, thankfully jerking me out of my head before I could be caught daydreaming about Beth. The guys might be acting semi-cool about the news of my relationship with her, but if I was caught mooning over my woman, the shit-giving would be relentless.

And yeah, maybe they were being cool because I'd been fucked up by Monica, so they were treading cautiously. But, also *yeah*, I was going to take advantage of the kindness.

It wouldn't last long.

The teasing would eventually commence, and I'd need to buck up, dish out, and deal.

For now, I'd enjoy the break.

And for the record, Cas didn't seem to disagree with Smitty's list, but...he also wasn't about to let our teammate play matchmaker either, saying, "Let's talk about Raph and—"

"Ready to move out, boys," Roger—our equipment manager —called, popping his head into the room, letting us know the bus was out front, ready to take us to the airport.

The man really did have perfect timing.

I shrugged into my jacket, picked up my bag, and tossed it over my shoulder, the locker room fading, the gossip and teasing less of a concern.

Because the bus being ready meant we' be on a plane soon.

Which meant we'd be home soon.

Which meant I'd be with Beth soon.

Which meant—

Smitty caught my arm as I moved past him.

Then the second miracle of the night happened—Smitty spoke quietly. "I know I asked you if you were sure before." A breath. "But I see it now."

"See what?"

"See what you can both give each other."

Oddly touched, I sucked in a breath.

A smirk. "And really, I'm just glad you got your head out of your ass."

Now *that* was a typical Smitty compliment.

But it was still one of the best I had ever received.

THIRTY

Beth

I WAS EXHAUSTED.

Always exhausted, though it wasn't from growing two babies.

I was exhausted because I'd just finished talking with Marin.

My first session.

God, it had been painful.

Sitting there in silence, trying to find the right way to get started, to explain. But how did I begin to unpack the decades of demons and the castle I'd built and how it had lasted for years but was threatening to crumple under my blossoming hope?

How did I explain that I was certain I was going to ruin my relationship with Raph? Be too broken, impossible to fix, the missing pieces too insurmountable?

How did I admit to only allowing myself to be with Raph

because I'd initially convinced myself that *I* was fixing *him*, but when in actuality, it felt very much the opposite?

How did I—

So much to unpack.

And that was without even dredging up the worst of it.

What I worried most about was telling Raph, telling *anyone*. Because...the one time I *had* talked about it—

I shuddered, and it rippled through my sore muscles, made my head throb anew.

I'd been so, so tense...and then Marin had asked me an innocuous question. I didn't even remember what it was, just that it had seemed to pop the cork on my words and then we were talking.

And I was *talking*.

Mostly about the present, explaining about the babies and Pru and Marcel. Talking about the date with Raph and how it was the first time in as long as I could remember that I wanted to stop hiding—and wanted it intensely enough to be willing to share the bad stuff that might turn him from me.

But—

Maybe the urge to share came now because Raph *wouldn't* turn from me.

Because he'd traveled his own tough path and I hadn't cut ties.

Of course, his shitty childhood wasn't his own fault, not like mine—

"Want to talk about it?"

Warm arms around my middle, a head resting gently on my shoulder. I leaned to the side and glanced up at Raph. My feet were in his hot tub, and he'd been at practice. A week since that date. A week since hope had blossomed.

Work and hockey games. Raph traveling for his, me hanging at my place and his for mine.

No more vertigo.

Lots of water—thanks to the calendar reminders Raph had set in my phone for me.

Loose clothes.

A growing belly.

And...safe and settled and *myself*. Raph's smiles and his laughter and his gentle hands. Raph's mouth and the glorious things it could do.

Raph's—

Just *Raph*.

So when I said, "No, not today, I think," it wasn't a surprise that his arms just tightened slightly, his chin returned to rest back on my shoulder, and he dipped his feet into the hot tub, thighs bracketing mine.

And when I said, "Tell me about Smitty's newest attempt at matchmaking," he obliged the change in topic.

Soon the past was gone—not buried, no longer encased in concrete...but its hooks weren't piercing me quite so deeply, those remaining demons peeking their heads out their doors perhaps not quite so terrifying.

Soon we were both laughing about Smitty's antics and Cas's protests and the way both had the locker room loose and relaxed and happy...and a betting pool had begun on how long it would take for Cas to fall.

The bets ranged from days to months.

But no years.

Hell, no one had even bet on it taking longer than six months for Smitty to fix Cas's picker and for Cas to fall head over feet for the perfect woman.

Romantics, all of them.

And I loved it, loved them, loved that the team was getting along.

All of which meant the team was playing great.

All of which meant that Raph was happy.

I was...getting there—or maybe that feeling growing in my belly, my heart, my mind was more than *getting* there.

Maybe I already *was* happy.

And maybe I could stay that way.

A MONTH LATER, Hazel, Pru, Kailey, and I were sitting at a high-top table at CeCe's.

A babysitter had been hired, seven more therapy sessions had been attended and survived and left me feeling wrung out...but in a good way. I was...dealing with it, dealing with the demons, the guilt, the worry, the past, and the pain. None of it was gone, but I was finally able to halt my thoughts, to redirect without burying.

And that felt like I'd shed a dozen pounds...all of which I was doing my level best to fill with cheese.

But my feeling wrung out meant that Raph, the lovable, overprotective lug, had decided to call an informal guys' night. Cas, Raph, Marcel, Oliver, Theo, Walker, and Smitty had all turned up and been relegated to another high-top table on the other side of the bar.

None of them minded.

The guys were...well, overprotective guys. Plus, they didn't cross the carefully drawn boundaries that I had laughingly put into place, sealing the declaration by laying a kiss on Raph that I knew had ensured we'd be all aboard the Breakers' gossip train.

I didn't mind that either.

I was feeling...protective and possessive myself.

But those feelings didn't send me spiraling, so... progress.

Then it had been time to stop thinking and to start participating in a much-needed Cheese Night Extravaganza.

Fried mozzarella. Nachos. Cheesy tater tots. Chili cheese fries. A nod at pretending to be healthy with a Caprese salad. Grilled cheese sliders.

If it had cheese, it went in our mouths.

As I went at the cheese consumption for a bit, though my belly was happy, I could cop to missing the ability to have a beer. God, all that cheese would go just perfectly with the hoppy deliciousness of an ice-cold beer.

"I'll bring you one in the delivery room," Pru said, my friend seeming to have understood exactly what me staring longingly at the pitcher of beer had brought to mind.

I cackled. "We've clearly been friends too long."

"Not long enough," Pru whispered, squeezing my hand. "Lucky to have you, Bethie."

I inhaled, eyes prickling. "You going gushy on me again?"

Pru's mouth turned up. "Let's just say that the next friends' trip we take is to a spa." A beat, her next words sounding like chewing on broken glass because they would be torture for Pru. "With *lots* of shopping expeditions." I let loose a squee that had Pru groaning, her head tipping back, eyes on the ceiling as she muttered, "Heaven help me."

I flung an arm around Pru and hugged her tight, and as I turned back to the table, I caught sight of Raph watching me, lips turned up at the corners.

"God, he's pretty," I whispered.

"I think he thinks the same of you," Pru whispered back.

"I think...I think I'm happy," I said softly.

A pause...long enough to draw my gaze back to Pru's, and I sucked in a breath when I saw that my friend's eyes were damp. "I'm glad, Bethie. So glad."

I sniffed.

Pru sniffed.

"Shit," Pru whispered. "We're both getting soft, aren't we?"

"I think we've both *been* soft all along." I nudged my shoulder against Pru's. "We just didn't recognize it."

Pru was quiet for a long time.

Then she nudged me back. "*Two* beers in the delivery room."

I grinned and when I looked up and saw Raph still watching me, I knew that I didn't *think* I was happy.

I *was*.

Then I saw who Cas was staring at, who he'd stared at more often than not over the years I'd known him...and I decided to play a bit of matchmaker herself...by convincing Jules to take her break at our table.

Class. Sass. Ass.

That was the perfect combination for Cas.

THIRTY-ONE

Raph

I KNEW Beth was up to mischief when my watch buzzed with a text and it was just a GIF that said,

> "Come here…and bring your friends."

I glanced up and she was smiling at me. Then she tilted her head slightly to the side.

To Jules.

Who was wearing her CeCe's shirt, but clearly on break, a soda in front of her and a cheese stick in her hand.

Which told me exactly how highly the girls thought of Jules.

Not just anyone could join in on the spoils of Cheese Night Extravaganza.

Hell, I'd almost lost a finger a time or two trying to steal a fry or chip or mozzarella stick, and I kind of thought they liked me.

Beth—seemingly not liking the delay—widened her eyes at me, tilting her head slightly more toward Jules...and then turning her gaze to Cas before returning it to mine, those widened eyes telling me to *get a clue.*

Jules.

Cas.

Oh yeah, now I liked *that.*

Except...if it went bad, then we wouldn't be able to show our faces at CeCe's again and Cheese Night Extravaganzas would be no more...not to mention the draft beers we all liked and—

Another buzz at my wrist.

Trust me?

Since that wasn't in question, cheese or beer or otherwise, I stood up, said, "Girl's night is over," and moved across the space, weaving between tables until I was behind Beth, shifting her hair to the side and inhaling deeply before pressing a kiss to the back of her neck.

"Did you just smell me?" she asked lightly.

A kiss to her cheek. "Yup." My lips to her ear. "And, for the record, you smell good."

She grinned. "I'll accept that."

I kept my lips on her ear. "Jules?"

"Decided to play matchmaker myself," she whispered, turning her head so her lips brushed mine. "Mostly because Cas can never take his eyes off her."

I'd missed that.

But as I glanced to the side, I saw Cas join us at the table... directly across from Jules and not being shy about watching her as she told a story about her son, his kindergarten teacher, and the confusion between diaphragm and digraph.

I chuckled, as did the rest of the table.

But Cas didn't.

His gaze was glued to Jules.

And I also supposed that could be why the woman Cas had been dating might have been more than a little pissed about Cas *just talking* to Jules.

"I'm seeing that," I whispered, nuzzling her throat.

"So"—she flashed me a grin—"I'm giving Smitty a run for his money with his matchmaking."

I stroked a finger down her cheek. "You giving him a run for his money in *anything* isn't even a question."

"Aw," Beth said, turned her head and pressing a kiss to my palm.

"Well," Jules said then, picking up her empty soda glass and sliding out of her seat—and I didn't miss that she seemed to be deliberately avoiding looking at Cas. "I should get back to work before Matt gets pissed at me for slacking off."

"What does Matt do when he gets pissed?"

It was a quiet question.

But Cas's voice had taken on a dangerous edge.

One that I had only heard in rare instances when an opposing player was being a total asshole on the ice.

Jules stilled, and her gaze finally went to Cas's.

The air tightened.

I found myself holding my breath, and Beth seemed to be doing the same.

But then Jules's responding laugh was soft. "He scowls at me. Matt is a good guy." She glanced away and nodded to the rest of the table, smile seeming as though it was a bit frayed on the edges. "Okay, then." A tap to the table. "I'll just make my rounds and then come back to close you guys out."

"Thanks, honey," Beth said, squeezing Jules's forearm. "No rush."

A glance to Cas, but then back to Beth and me, her expression warming, that smile turning genuine. "Yeah, I'll bet you don't mind cozying up to your hot hockey player."

Beth laughed, leaned back against me. "Nope. Don't mind that at all."

With a grin, Jules slipped away.

Smitty bent, sticking his head in between ours, forcing us apart, his features fixed in a narrow-eyed glare. "Trying to take my job, Bethie?"

Beth blew on and then buffed her knuckles on her shoulder. "I think that glare and your question both speak of insecurity." A beat, lips turning up. "Mostly because I'm doing a better job."

Smitty growled, but then he surprised me *and* Beth, too—seemingly—by pressing a kiss to her cheek and straightening. "All right gents and ladies, Cheese Night Extravaganza is on me this time."

"Smitty—" Beth began. "You don't—"

"On me," he repeated, rounding the table, and slinging an arm around Kailey's shoulder. "Now, all of you beat it so that I can pick up my woman in a bar."

Kailey blushed but just leaned back against Smitty, added, "One of you guys can get next time."

Quiet where he was loud.

But smart, strong, and with a steel backbone. We all knew she battled social anxiety, so her speaking up now was something we weren't going to ignore.

"Okay, Kay," Hazel said in her usual gentle tone, looping her arm through Oliver's and leaning on him slightly in a way that told me she might have had one too many beers.

Pru was doing the same to Marcel.

But my Bethie, obviously, was sober.

She still leaned her body against mine, though, and I might

not know all of her yet, but I knew enough, *felt* enough. "Come on, love," she murmured, yawning, before rising on tiptoe. "Let's go home and give Smitty his time for his reconnaissance."

Love.

I smiled.

"Let's go home."

Her ass was pressing into my cock.

And I was trying to be good.

But it was pressing, rocking and rolling against my pelvis... and I was hard, growing harder by the second.

So, I was thinking about stats and not the soft sounds that were coming out of Beth's parted lips.

Not the fact that she was dreaming about me, and that dream was hot.

How did I know this?

Because she'd also been talking in her sleep.

And some of the things she'd said included my name and a plea for me to fuck her.

Christ.

"Raph," she moaned, head falling back against my shoulder, hips pressing hard, and—

I couldn't help it.

I thrust forward, one hand gripping the curve of her hip, drawing me into her, and I couldn't stifle my groan.

But it had barely crossed my lips before Beth went still.

Fuck.

"Shh, honey. Sleep."

Her back arched, ass rubbing against me, and—

Fuck.

"Raph?"

"Go to sleep, baby."

She rubbed again. "What if I don't want to?"

I inhaled sharply. "It's late and you're tired—"

Another arch of her back. "I'm not feeling so tired anymore."

"No?" I asked, dropping my head, dragging my lips along her throat.

Her hand slipped between us, wrapped around my cock. "No, honey. I'm not tired."

I stopped thinking right around the point her fingers slid under the material of my underwear and landed on my bare skin, but I *definitely* stopped thinking when she pushed me back, clambered on top and tore my T-shirt that she'd commandeered over her head, dropping it to the side.

Breasts.

Fuck, her breasts made me crazy.

I sat up, cupping one in my palm, guiding it to my mouth, sucking deeply on her nipple.

"Raph!" she gasped.

Then I was...undone.

Suckling both breasts, dragging my lips and tongue along her jaw, her throat, nipping on her earlobe, rearing back to kiss her deeply. Dragging her beneath me, kissing down along her ribs, softly over the top of her growing belly, then *down*.

Tugging her underwear off.

I pressed my face to her pussy and inhaled deeply. "You smell fucking good here too, sugarpie."

She shuddered, cried out when I thrust my tongue into her folds. But I didn't stop, just fucked her with my fingers and my tongue until she was crying out again, this time because she was coming. And then I was inside her, stroking probably too fast and too hard, but she had wrapped her legs around my waist, and I was cupping her breasts, rolling her nipples.

Eyes half-mast.

Lips swollen and parted.

Neck arched.

Skin sheened with sweat.

"Oh God," she whispered. "Oh God. There. Right—*oh*—"

She bucked beneath me, pussy convulsing so tightly I saw stars...and then I wasn't seeing anything.

Because my orgasm was rippling through me, sucking me dry, and it was taking everything in me to not collapse on top of her.

Chest heaving, brain muddled, I managed to roll us to the side.

And then we lay there, quiet as our breathing slowed.

I didn't realize that tension had crept into me until she rested a hand on my chest. "I'm fine, love. Promise."

There that was again.

Love.

The tension left me.

"Okay, sugarpie."

Her lips curved, eyes closing, and she snuggled into me. "It's getting better. *I'm* getting better."

But she hadn't shared all the demons.

And though I was trying to be patient, though I understood she needed to come to terms with her past on her own timeline —and I was so fucking proud that she was working so hard on doing it over the last month—in these moments, it was killing me.

She'd given enough that I knew her past was heavy.

Heavy enough for me to want to shoulder its weight.

But how could I if she didn't give me the rest?

And how could I ask if she wasn't ready?

And how could I just fall asleep without knowing for sure she was okay?

And how—

She fell asleep, soft, slow breaths puffing on my throat, and I knew that answered one of my questions, at least for the moment.

How to fall asleep?

After she was safely ensconced in her dreams.

THIRTY-TWO

Beth

I CLICKED OFF THE TV, my skin itching.

The Breakers had won again.

The playoffs were beginning in just days.

And...he wasn't sleeping.

Raph wasn't sleeping.

He was playing well, consistent and solid, like always. But with none of the flair and creativity and *drive* that he'd had for the entirety of the regular season.

Minus the last weeks.

Because that had been slowly drying up.

Because he wasn't sleeping.

He was worried about me. I knew that. And I had the means to solve it.

I needed to tell him.

I *had* needed to tell him for the last months.

But I'd been putting it off because...well, for *all* the reasons I had. All of which Marin had helped me understand weren't particularly valid. They were excuses and fears and ways for me to hold tight to those barriers I'd erected.

Because Raph wasn't like them.

He'd proved it to me time and again.

And now, the fact that I was holding tight to my fears was impacting him.

So...it was time.

I pushed off my couch, moved to my bedroom, pretending that it was still walking, when it was really waddling, and grabbed a bag, started filling it with my loose clothes—though they were definitely a whole lot *less* loose than they'd been when I bought them.

Luckily, my blood pressure was stable, the twins were growing, and I was mostly feeling good.

Very pregnant, but good.

The doctors were shooting for a full thirty-six weeks to give the babies as much time as possible to grow and their lungs to mature.

Eight more weeks.

Boy, was I counting the days down.

Though, I might have to buy another wardrobe if my belly kept growing at the rate it was.

More shopping.

I grinned. *Oh, the humanity.*

Laughing to myself, I moved into my bathroom and grabbed my toiletries then headed down the stairs and snagged my laptop and charger, tucking them into my overnight bag. But just after I'd shoved my feet into shoes and was pulling out my phone, intending to book a train ticket up to D.C. so that I could catch up with Raph in the city before their next road game, my doorbell rang.

Frowning, I moved into the entryway, peeking out the side-light and seeing...Hazel on my porch.

"What?" I whispered and quickly, I reached for the knob, turning the lock, and tugging open the door.

Hazel moved into me, close enough that worry began coiling in my belly, her gaze flicking down to my feet, her eyes flickering and tension entering her frame. Then she leaned to the side, seeing—presumably—the overnight bag on the bench in the hall where I had left it.

"I knew you were going to do this."

I blinked at the tone. It wasn't soft and gentle, not at all like Hazel. "Knew I was going to..." I began.

"Cut your losses and run."

What the—

I was pregnant with her other best friend's babies. I'd bought a house here. I had a job, friends, a life. I had...Raph.

"Why would I run?"

Hazel took my hand, drew me away from the door, like she was seriously worried that I was going to sprint out into the night and disappear. But her voice softened as she tugged me down onto the couch. "Beth, honey, I know we haven't talked about that night, and I've been trying to give you space to cope with everything, especially since you mentioned to me that you were talking with Marin."

Pru and Hazel both knew I was in therapy.

It wasn't like I was going to keep it a secret—not after Hazel had been there in the hospital, certainly not with Pru's babies in my belly.

"But I've watched you over the last couple of weeks..."

She had?

Of course, Hazel had.

"Honey," I began.

"And the last time you got like this, you told Pru and me you were busy with work, and then we didn't hear from you for six months."

I frowned. "I've never gone more than a week without talking to one or both of you since college."

"You picked up when we called, texted back when we started the conversation, but you didn't once call first or text first or email first, honey, and oftentimes any replies to our messages were a long time in coming, and you know it."

I wanted to deny it.

Just immediately and out of hand.

But...breathe, think, then reflect.

I did that, and it didn't take long for me to come to the conclusion. "You're right," I murmured.

Hazel blinked.

"But here's the thing, honey. I know I haven't shared every-thing—" I stopped, shook my head. "I know that I've hardly shared *anything*. And I know that I owe you an explanation, but I'm leaving."

"Bethie—" Hazel began.

"To go to Raph."

Another blink from her friend.

"Yeah, honey. I know I haven't been open like I should have. God, you and Pru. You two were the only lights I allowed in my life for such a long time, and I still didn't give you everything—"

"You don't owe either of us an explanation—"

"Maybe not, but if I'm using it as an excuse to keep you guys from getting too close then, yeah, I do." I sighed. "Because it also means that if I stop concreting over the demons instead of just dealing with them, then maybe they won't have so much power over me."

Hazel's face gentled. "That sounds like a solid thought." A flicker of guilt through her expression. "I'm—"

Our fingers were still linked together, so I gently squeezed Hazel's hand, cutting her off before she could apologize.

"This isn't your fault."

"My job is *literally* to see these kinds of things," Hazel whispered. "And I missed it." Her throat worked, more guilt. "And then I misread you again this week."

I tugged my hand free, used both to cup Hazel's cheeks. "I had a lifetime to bury my shit, honey."

"I—"

"And you do not get to take on my trauma. I know it's your superpower, fixing things—"

Hazel snorted. "Pot meet kettle."

"Okay, I know *our* superpower is to fix everything."

Hazel smiled. Finally.

So I added, "But I'm learning that not everything needs to be fixed."

Hazel closed her eyes, sighed softly.

"Sometimes dings and cracks are okay," I whispered. "Because it's better than slapping on a veneer and pretending that everything is perfect."

Scratches and dents and warm and *lived*-in were so much better than an empty, pristine castle with a concreted-over basement. Even with demons in the basement and doors that may never close properly and drafts and probably a few ghosts in the attic.

"Yeah," Hazel whispered. "It is."

"You okay?" I whispered back.

"No." Still whispering. "My best friend was hurting for years, I missed it, and now she's gone on and gotten healthy all on her own." Her lids slid open. "And I'm so damned proud of her for it."

Shit.

Now I was going to cry.

"Haze," I murmured.

"I love you."

Yup. Definitely going to cry. Mush paired with pregnancy hormones?

Total sob fest.

But hell, it was worth it, especially when I was able to wrap my arms around Hazel and hug her tightly...or as tightly as my giant belly allowed.

Eventually, though, I knew I needed to get to Raph.

"I've got to buy a train ticket, honey," I whispered long moments later.

"Right," Hazel said. "Load your butt into my car." She stood up, reached for my bag. "You can buy one while I drive you to the station."

The lights were on in my castle.

The door was unlocked.

There were plush rugs on the floor.

And the kitchen sink was filled with dishes, there were crumbs on the carpet of the living room, and a glass was leaving a ring on her coffee table.

It was *home*. Finally.

And...it was perfect.

THIRTY-THREE

Raph

IT WAS LATE, and we'd barely made it to our hotel rooms. All I wanted to do was call Beth, make sure she was good, and then go to bed.

But as I laid out my toiletries in the bedroom, my cell glued to my ear, ringing through on Beth's number—and then her voicemail—worry began growing in my stomach.

Truthfully, it didn't take much.

That worry had been souring my gut for weeks now.

Beth seemed okay, but as more time went on and she didn't share, the knots in my belly tightened and grew, twisting and sitting heavy. She'd seemed okay before. Seemed free and loose and happy—all of what she was exhibiting now—and then I'd had to drive her to the hospital in the midst of a panic attack, talking about demons and ultimately needing sedation.

She'd shared.

Some.

I knew about her mom and her marriages, about the abuse

and the money in her trust fund. I knew why she'd gone into the work she did—charities for women and children who were in need or in abusive relationships.

But she hadn't given me *all* of it.

And I was trying to be patient.

But it was fucking *killing* me.

I hung up without leaving a message, finished setting out my shit for the morning, did my business in the bathroom, and then typed out a text.

No reply.

And when I went back in a few minutes later, knowing I was obsessing when she'd probably just fallen asleep, I saw that she'd read the message a few minutes before.

Read, but hadn't replied.

That sour feeling grew.

Trying to ignore it, I typed out another message.

That was left on read, too.

Hand clenching into a fist at my side, I decided to fuck it and just called her again. I'd apologize if I woke her up, but if she was awake, I would feel better hearing her voice.

Except, she didn't pick that call up either.

"Fuck," I whispered, trying to sort out what to do.

But even as I was doing that, there was a knock on my door.

"Fuck," I muttered again, moving toward the peephole.

One glance had my eyes widening, and then I was tearing open the door. "Beth." My voice was a rasp, and I hauled her toward me, gaze scouring every inch of her, trying to make sure she was okay. "What's wrong—why—?"

Her bag hit the carpet; her arms came around my middle. "Hi, love," she whispered.

"Why are you here?"

That came out brusquely, which was totally not what I'd

intended, but she was in another state in the middle of the night and—

"Breathe, honey." Another whisper. A gentle one this time. "Everything is good with me."

I placed my hand over her belly, which had grown to crazy proportions in the time we'd been together, and with still two more months (hopefully) to go, it was only going to get bigger. "Are they—?"

"They're fine, too."

Relief sliding through me.

Her hand came to my jaw. "But you're not."

I inhaled. "Sugarpie, I'm fine—"

"You're not, baby, and I know why."

My stomach began churning. "Bethie—"

"You're not, and it's because of me."

She was, quite literally, the best thing that had happened to me. I hadn't been this happy, this settled *ever*.

"I should have told you the rest, and I should have told you it a while ago."

"You don't need to—"

"You're in this with me. It affects me. Which means it affects you."

I didn't have an argument for that.

So, I didn't protest when she took my hand and drew me to the bed, sitting on the edge and patting next to her.

I sank down at her side.

"You know my stepdad was abusive." Anger prickled down my spine. "But you don't know that for a long time, I felt like I was the bigger monster."

She shuddered, and I slid up the bed, gathering her into my lap. "You're not a monster."

Silence, then, "I'm finally starting to realize that." Her head tilted back, her blue eyes tinged with pain.

"Sugarpie," I whispered.

Her shoulders rose and fell on a breath. "He hit her. A lot. And if I got in the middle of it or was in the wrong place at the wrong time...then I got hit, too."

I knew that, but I struggled to keep my body loose, to not tense up.

She needed me calm.

"I don't know how exactly she managed it, but Mom convinced me to go to boarding school, made it seem like it was my idea." She sighed. "I remember overhearing part of the conversation, but it wasn't until she told me later that it would be better for me that I realized what I'd heard wasn't her trying to get rid of me, but rather her trying to get me safe."

"She was protecting you."

"Yeah."

A long pause, her body settling more heavily against mine, as though she were soaking up my strength and warmth and that, more than anything else, had the twisting in my insides settling, the sourness fading.

"I wanted to go," she whispered. "That was bad enough. I wanted to get away from the yelling, from his fists."

I smoothed a hand down her spine. "I think anyone would want to, honey."

"I was relieved."

That was pained.

"I was relieved that I wouldn't get yelled at or hit anymore. I was relieved that *my mom* would take that instead." A breath. "I was relieved I didn't have to walk on eggshells or hide in the dark corner of my room or *hear* her get hit."

"Baby," I whispered.

"I was relieved that I was free."

"I think that's normal, honey."

"Yeah." A breath. "I didn't tell anyone."

"What?"

"I didn't tell anyone what was happening at home, not my grandparents, not my teachers, not my counselors at school, not my friends. I didn't tell *anyone*."

"Did your stepfather threaten you if you did tell?"

Cold in those pale blue eyes. "Of course, he did."

I clenched my jaw. "Then it's not surprising you didn't tell."

"Yeah," she whispered. "But I felt guilty about it for a long time. If I'd just said *something,* then things might have turned out differently." She sighed. "But I didn't say anything, and while the guilt is still there and probably always will be, what came after was worse."

I braced.

"So, I was relieved to be free of him, guilty to have not told anyone. She called. A lot. And I remember being so annoyed that she kept bugging me, kept making me go down to the office to take her calls when I was at school. I think she was trying to assure herself that I was okay, but I felt like she was trying to take away the only bit of normal I had, and I was a kid with my first taste of freedom in my life and...I was annoyed with my mom who'd risked everything to get me out of that house." She swallowed hard. "And I know she risked everything because then—then he killed her."

"Oh, baby," I whispered, arms tightening.

"He beat her to death, Raph. Hit her so hard that her face wasn't—" Beth's voice broke. "Well, it wasn't her face any longer when I saw it at the hospital, and they blamed me." Her voice broke again, and she sounded close to tears, so I just held her tight, running my hand up and down her back and waited for her to be ready to go on.

But when she didn't speak, I asked gently, "Who blamed you, sugarpie?"

"My grandparents." A breath. "The police."

Fucking *hell.*

"My grandparents...fuck"—she blew out a breath—"I remember the expression on their faces when they realized I knew what was happening, and that I didn't do *something* about it. God, the disgust and anger and—that stung so much, and seeing that I knew—*knew*—I'd done wrong. It was *my* fault that she was dead. *My.* Fault." Rage was burning through me, but I tamped it down. "And then, when the detective looked at me like that, too...well, that fact burned itself on my soul. I *knew* it was my fault. I knew I was as big of a monster as I was because otherwise, why would my grandparents look at me like that? Why would the detective? It was me. *I* was the monster. I-I—" She broke off, and I buried my head in her hair, holding her tight, breathing slowly so that I didn't add to her distress.

"It wasn't your fault," I murmured.

"I know," she said softly, so softly that I could barely hear it considering my pulse was pounding in my ears as I strived for control. "It took me a long time to get there. *Too* long." She lifted her head and sighed. "So that's my secret, that's the horrible, ugly demon in the basement of my soul, the one I tried to bury time and again—it was *my* fault my mom was dead. Because I might as well have killed her myself. Because me being happy to go to school, happy to pretend what was happening at home *wasn't* actually happening. And then me being annoyed she was calling, and my grandparents and that detective—" A shake of her head. "I was young. It implanted itself deep. And I was punishing myself because I thought I deserved it. Doubly so when he managed to hire lawyers that got him off, when he didn't even have to *pay* for doing that for her."

"Sugarpie," I croaked, taking her cheeks in my hands, and gently kissing her forehead. "God, honey, I'm so sorry."

She leaned in. "Me too."

I stroked a hand through her hair.

"So now you know everything." She took a breath, released it slowly. "And now you need to stop worrying about me."

I froze, leaned back enough to meet her eyes. "What?"

"You've been letting my past eat at you, and I spent too long doing that to myself, and I love you too much to let you do that and—"

I'd frozen before.

But now I went *absolutely* still.

"—I haven't come this far, *you* haven't come this far for us to let it impact our future. And I'm not going to therapy and working my ass off to get my head straight, only for you to have yours—"

"Sugarpie?"

Her words stopped coming, but her lips remained parted.

"You love me?"

Her eyes widened. "I—" Her teeth pressed into her bottom lip then that red-painted mouth tipped up, and she shrugged. "Yeah, love, I think I made that clear when I shared my mozzarella sticks with you all those months ago."

She'd been calling me *love* for a while.

I'd noticed but hadn't taken it in. Not what it really meant.

Not what all of *it* meant—the cheese sharing, the smiles, the sex, the time together, the therapy, and smiling at me through the glass at games, and shopping. Her staying up late and texting me when I got to hotels, learning about opponents, and giving me advice from Eva Moreno's sports blog. Her hand in mine, her body pressed close, her mouth on my skin.

All of it.

So much.

And I was fucking greedy for more.

I wanted a lifetime of *more*.

"Fuck, I love you, sugarpie," I groaned, wrapping my arms around her, and holding her tight.

"Yeah?" she whispered.

"Yeah, love," I said. "I think I've made that clear when I shared my—"

Her hands went to my shoulders, mouth dropping close to my, breath on my lips.

"Your life," she supplied.

"*Our* life," I corrected.

A red-lipped smile that settled like a balm in my belly. "Our life," she repeated.

And then...she kissed me.

And then...I felt as though my life had finally begun.

THIRTY-FOUR

Beth

"I'M OKAY, LOVE. I PROMISE."

His eyes did that thing they did when I called him that.

Warm Caribbean ocean.

White sand beaches.

Hot, humid air on my skin.

A cocktail in my hand, my sexy shirtless male next to me.

"We're going on vacation once I can have a Mai Tai," I commanded.

He grinned, smoothed his hand over my cheek. "Sure you're good?"

We were standing in one of the tunnels of the arena, an elevator nearby, ready to take me up to the concourse and the seat I'd park my ass in to watch the game.

Then Raph had gotten permission for me to take the plane home with him.

And we'd be back in Baltimore.

Back to our lives.

I couldn't wait.

For the first time ever, my life was uncomplicated and light, and I was *happy*.

Happy!

So yeah, I rose on tiptoe, brushed my lips over his, nudged him back. "I'm about to watch my man play hockey." Another nudge. "So, I'm sure I'm good." I watched him struggle, not wanting to leave me, and, no lie, that warmed my heart. But he needed to get ready for the game, so I added, "I expect two goals tonight."

A smirk. "That's all?"

My hand down his chest, sliding over his skintight undershirt that cupped every muscle in a way that had me wanting to coax him down the hall and find an empty room to show him exactly how much I liked it.

But...work.

Alas.

He had it.

"Two goals," I chirped, tossing my hair over my shoulder. "That's all."

And then I brushed my lips to his again and waddled to the elevator, waving to him just before the doors closed.

His smile tucked its way into my heart.

Or maybe painted itself onto a giant canvas which magically hung itself over the hearth in m castle's family room.

Either way, it was perfect.

THE CROWD GROANED, but I was cheering.

Because Raph had just surpassed my challenge.

A hat trick.

He winked at me as he skated by. No *sugarpies* through the glass because I was about twelve rows back.

But still close enough to see that smile, that wink, to toss a hat that bounced off my shoulder onto the ice to join the couple of others trickling down to celebrate Raph's hat trick. I'd known my impromptu trip to DC had been worth it about ten seconds into his first shift.

He was back.

And I...was someone new.

The inside matching the outside for the first time ever.

Grinning, I watched the Breakers trounce their opponents, the crowd thinning as the deficit in score increased, and even though I hated to waste a minute, the babies had decided to play trampoline on my bladder.

So, at the next whistle, I hefted myself out of my seat, grabbed my purse, and waddled my ass up the long, long staircase.

Out of breath, I took a minute to just suck in air at the top, watching as the puck dropped down below and Walker began leading his line on a drive up the ice.

"Excuse me?"

I whirled, realized I was blocking most of the top of the stairs. "Oh, I'm sorry," I told the woman who'd come up next to me, two young boys at her side. "Here," I said, "You take my spot. I'm leaving anyway."

"Oh, please don't."

Okay, that was weird.

"Um," I glanced at the usher whose gaze was on the game far below.

"Please stay."

Yeah. This was giving me all sorts of vibes...and not any of them were good.

I backed up a step, debating on whether I should move back

down the stairs or just sidle away and use my pass to take the elevator back downstairs.

A glance down to the boys at her side. "Please."

"I'm sorry, I really should go."

"How is he?"

I frowned.

"My boy." A beat. "How is he?"

That was the moment my heart began pounding, thudding against my ribcage.

That was the moment I decided to stop trying to be polite and turned to leave.

A hand gripping my arm tightly halted me.

Slowly, I spun back to face them, glancing from the boys—whose focus was still on the game—back up to the woman.

There was something...almost familiar about her, something that pinged into the back of my mind, something that prickled along my spine.

"Let go of me," I said carefully, taking a step back, away from the top of the stairs, away from the woman, even though she still gripped my wrist. Which meant that my arm was now awkwardly stretched out.

But hopefully making clear to anyone who so much as glanced at me that I was not happy about this contact.

"Let go of me," I said louder.

Loud enough that the usher turned to us, concern entering the slender blond woman's face. "Excuse me, are you okay?"

"I'd like her to let go of me—" I began.

The fingers on my arm tightened. "You need to bring him back to us." My body jerked as the woman yanked at my arm. "You need to have him talk to me."

The usher stepped closer, pulled out her radio.

"Who?"

"My Raphael. You need to get him to talk to me. Not for me. For my boys—"

Boys who were now distracted from the ice and staring at me and their mother and—

The woman jerked my arm again, hard enough to send pain shooting up that arm. "You *have* to," she said, leaning close enough that I could see every line in her face, could see every shade of blue in her eyes.

Her. Eyes.

And that was when I put the pieces together.

And that was when...my happy disappeared.

THIRTY-FIVE

Raph

SHE WASN'T WAITING at the bottom of the elevator like we'd arranged.

My hair was wet. I'd skipped out of the locker room as soon as I could...and she wasn't there.

I grabbed my cell from my pocket and jabbed the button to call the elevator.

Worry was back, clenching my insides.

All I knew was that I needed to get up there. She needed me, and I had to be there. I jabbed at the button again, using my other hand to dial her number.

It rang and rang.

Voicemail.

"Fuck," I hissed, jabbing the button a third time.

"Um, Raph?"

I turned, saw Cas was there. "What?" I snapped.

"I think you need to come—"

The elevator doors opened.

"No, I don't." I stepped onto the car.

"Beth is—"

Knots in my insides.

I clamped my hand on the metal door, stopping it from sliding closed. "Beth is what?"

Cas's face was grave. "She's down the hall, man."

I was moving before I realized, in Cas's face, my hand gripping my friend's shirt. "Where?" I growled.

Cas, thankfully, didn't get hackles up and snap back.

He just pointed to the right.

I let go then hauled ass down the hall, aware that Cas was following me, but not focusing on that.

Because...Beth.

Something wasn't right with Beth. I felt it in my belly. I knew it because she wasn't at the elevators, because Cas's face, his voice, they weren't right.

"Where?" I snapped when the hall split off into two directions.

"Left," Cas said.

I spun to the left, my intestines in fucking knots...

And then I saw her.

Leaning against the wall, her neck bent, gaze on her feet.

"Beth, honey—" I took her hands, dipping down when she jumped, trying to see her face. But she didn't make me wait, just glanced up, and her eyes were stark.

"Raph, I need to—"

The door behind her opened.

And...my mom stepped out.

"What the fuck?" I whispered.

"She...um...found me inside the arena," Beth said carefully. "She—"

A slender woman in a fitted jacket stepped out of the room,

a security guard at her shoulder. "Do you know this woman?" the guard asked.

Tempting to say no.

But prevaricating wouldn't get us any closer to sorting out whatever the fuck this shit show was about.

"My mother," I gritted out.

The security guard nodded.

The woman next to me, the one in the jacket, said, "She accosted your wife. Grabbed her arm and wouldn't let go even though your wife asked several times."

My hold on my temper had been markedly thin.

Two fucking decades without one word aside from asking me through my social media to show her boys the Cup, and then to show up in my life like this? Hurting my woman? Making a scene at my place of work?

Beth's hand found my, squeezed. "Breathe, love. I'm okay."

"Where did she grab you?"

Maybe it spoke to how on the edge I was, but Beth didn't argue, just held up her arm. "Here. See? I'm okay, love."

No marks. No bruises. No scrapes or fingerprints. And *love* on Beth's tongue.

I breathed.

"Come on," I said. "We're going."

Beth squeezed my hand again. "There are two boys with her. Your half-brothers."

Shit. *Show.*

I stopped, gaze hitting the ceiling.

Fucking hell.

"Sir, what do you want—"

"You're our favorite player," a small voice whispered.

My gaze jerked down, and I saw that a boy who was maybe ten or eleven had peeked around the doorway.

Beth's hand went tight.

"Yeah"—another boy popped his head out, this one younger, maybe seven or eight—"Mom said that we might be great hockey players like you one day if we practice hard enough."

I clenched my jaw, and I wanted nothing more than to fuck off out of here.

But...these kids weren't my mother.

They had no fucking clue. How could they?

"Yeah, buddy," I said. "You can."

I turned to my mother, sucked in a breath, and searched for anything remotely kind to say. What came out was, "Did you pick better this time?"

Guilt on her face, blue eyes like my own clouding with guilt. "Yes," she whispered.

That settled somewhere in me, a wound I hadn't even known still existed. "How long?"

"Fifteen years."

Fifteen.

And she'd left me with my father still. Left me and started over and—

I looked at the two boys in the doorway, thought of the abuse my father had put me through, the yelling, the neglect, the shit heaped on day after day, and then I thought about where it had gotten me, where I was today. The woman who was standing next to me, body pressed close, hand tight around mine.

And I waited for the rage to take me over, for the fury of the circumstances to cloud my mind.

But...it didn't come.

Instead, I was staring at two boys, at my half-brothers, and I was glad their childhood had been different from mine. Glad there was light in their eyes instead of shadows.

I was pissed that my mother had dared to lay a hand on Beth.

But that was it.

The rest was...indifference.

This woman had stopped being my mother when she walked out, when she stayed away. But my brothers? My brothers were innocent.

"Do they know?" A beat. "About me?"

My mother shook her head, whispered, "No."

I didn't know whether to be relieved or not.

I glanced down at Beth.

Her expression was placid, but I felt her tension.

And suddenly, it didn't matter what I felt. There would be time to unpack it later.

For now, I needed to take care of two boys who had nothing to do with this then get my woman and my ass on a plane.

"Raph?" Beth whispered.

"I'm okay." Another squeeze of her hand before I released her and moved to the boys, squatting down in front of them. "What are your names?"

"Mario," the older one said.

"Bennie," the younger one chimed.

"It's cool to meet you guys." Their faces lit up. "Do you come to a lot of games?"

"We got an eight-pack for Christmas!"

Tickets to eight games. The perfect gift for hockey-crazed kids.

"Wow," I said, meaning it, "that's awesome."

"And Mom lets us pick out a souvenir every time we come." Bennie held up a medium-sized plush of the team's mascot. "See?"

I smiled. "That's really cool."

"I gave Bennie my souvenir money because it was too

much," Mario whispered loudly. "He's gonna let me have his next time so I can get a T-shirt."

Good kids.

Happy kids.

I glanced up, saw hope in my mother's eyes then looked back down at Mario. "That sounds like a good plan."

"Now, I want to talk with you more," I told them, "but we have to catch a plane, so maybe your mom can give me her number and the next time you come down to Baltimore, you can come to a Breakers game."

"Really?" the boys exclaimed.

"Really," I said.

"Whoa," Bennie said.

"Awesome," Mario added, practically bouncing from foot to foot.

I held out my fist, bumped both of the boys'.

Then I stood, leaned close to my mother. "Devon Scott at Prestige Media Group is my agent. I'll tell him to expect a call from you."

Tears in her blue eyes.

"I'm sorry," she whispered.

The apology meant nothing because I...felt nothing—except no, it wasn't nothing. It was...neutral indifference.

"You'll make a great father," she went on, gaze going from Beth's stomach back to me.

"Thanks," I muttered, turning away from her, taking Beth's hand.

And then I started walking.

Away from my past.

Toward my future.

THIRTY-SIX

Beth

CAS GAVE me wide eyes before he turned and took the steps leading onto the plane.

I understood the unspoken message.

But I didn't think addressing Raph's mother showing up out of the blue, latching onto me, and crossing all kinds of boundaries was appropriate for a middle-of-the-night flight, after a road trip and a series of tough games, right before the playoffs.

"Up you go, sugarpie," Raph said, hands drifting to my waist and nudging me forward. "Get that hot ass of yours into a seat."

I didn't argue, just headed up, sat down, buckled in, and worried...

Fingers on my cheek.

"I'm fine."

"Raph, love, your mother just showed up after *years* of no

contact with your two half-brothers in tow and they say *you're* their favorite player and—"

"Is there shit for me to unpack?" he asked softly. "Fuck yeah. But is it tearing me up inside? No, sugarpie, it's not." He sighed, ran a hand through his hair, voice low. "Instead, I looked at that woman and knew she was no more my mother than Smitty is. Not anymore. The memories from my child-hood—the pictures, the recipes I still use, *those* were my mother. That woman back at the rink...she was a stranger."

I nibbled on my bottom lip. All of that sounded well-adjusted.

But...it had still been a lot.

His thumb gently freed my lip, smoothed over it. "I'm okay, I swear. And when I'm not, I know who'll have my back."

His eyes told me that he meant *I* would have his back and his teammates and Pru and Hazel and—

"I'm okay," he whispered. "And there comes a point that I'm not, I know you'll help me get there."

My heart squeezed and affection for my man filled every single one of my cells. Christ I loved him.

His mouth brushed mine.

And I was stepping into warm ocean water, feeling that humid breeze on my face.

A gentle hand on my cheek.

My lids peeling open to see Raph with clear, peaceful eyes and no pain lingering on the edges of his expression.

"Honey," I whispered.

He stroked a hand over my hair. "Yeah?"

"I love you."

His smile settled over me like that heated breeze. "Yeah, you do."

A swat to his shoulder.

His arm came around me, tugging me close. "I love you, too, sugarpie."

"Yeah, you do," I teased back.

And then I snuggled into my man and was asleep before we even hit cruising altitude.

HIS RAGE CAME two months later, well after the season was over.

After the Breakers were eliminated in the second round of the playoffs.

Painful as hell to bear witness to it, especially with my man and the other guys giving every single ounce of themselves on the ice and having it not be enough.

All that work...and then just *done*.

But I hadn't begrudged the extra time with Raph once the sadness had faded—sleeping together every night, hanging out and doing nothing. Movies and meals and cuddling and sex... having to use every bit of our creativity to make it work. And doing what we were doing that night, talking with our feet in the pool, staring up at the night sky.

Tonight he was talking, letting that anger out.

I was listening. I had his back.

And the fixer in me fucking *loved* that.

But the rest of me was—and been for weeks—just boiling every time I thought about it. Every time I wondered how in the fuck that woman could have left Raph behind.

An innocent boy.

Her boy.

Then to just start over, not bothering to come back for him.

Not bothering to call or reach out...until he could do something for *her*.

Because she'd called Raph's manager, of course she had.

And Raph, the good man that he was, had given the boys an experience to end all experiences—playoff tickets, jerseys, swag, meet and greets. They'd had the *works*, and the joy on their faces had been incredible.

Raph had done that.

He'd given them that joy.

And his mother hadn't done anything else. Not another apology—something better than *I'm sorry*. Not a word of thanks or an explanation for why she'd left Raph to his drunk, abusive father. Instead, she'd seemed uncomfortable around her oldest son, hovering around Mario and Bennie, and just fucking *taking*.

Me...well, I was infuriated by his mother, but I kept my anger under wraps.

Or so I had thought.

Because Raph trailed his fingers across my jaw. "My fierce defender."

I scowled.

He kissed me. "Like I said, so *freaking* fierce."

"You don't hurt my man," I whispered. "Not then. Not now."

"Considering I feel the same way about you, I'll let the overprotectiveness slide." I rolled my eyes, but he simply smiled and tugged at a lock of my hair. "Did I also mention beautiful?"

"That's you, my love. You're beautiful here." I covered his chest, the spot just over his heart, with my palm. Feeling the steady beating, knowing that it was mine, just as my heart was his. "And all mine."

"Possessive. Beautiful. Fierce. Strong." A kiss to my forehead, my nose, one cheek, the other, each punctuating a word. "And most important, *mine*."

"Who's possessive now?" I teased.

"Me. Definitely me." He shifted so that his legs were on either side of mine, arms wrapping around my middle.

"I get much bigger, you won't be able to do that."

A kiss to my shoulder, one palm resting on my belly, feeling the babies move, though they'd slowed a bit in recent days, space at an absolute premium.

"Beautiful," he murmured again, leaning around me, and pressing his mouth to my jaw.

Which happened to be the exact moment that my water broke.

A gush soaking both of our bottoms, dripping along the stones, *plinking* into the pool.

Turning, my wide eyes hit his, which were equally as wide.

"I'm guessing," I whispered as amniotic fluid kept dripping into the pool, "that means the pool guy is going to have to come rebalance the chemicals?"

His lips tipped up.

And then we were both laughing.

Laughter that lasted all of a second before a rippling pain trailed through my abdomen. "Holy hell," I whispered, bending over, gripping Raph's legs tightly until it passed.

"Right," he said once it was over. He glanced at his watch, and I knew he was clocking the time, would be tracking my contractions.

Because he was Raph.

Because he'd read books and blogs and watched videos, even though these weren't his babies.

Because he was going to be there for me every step of the way.

"I'm getting you upstairs for a quick change and to grab your bag"—I'd had it packed for weeks now—"while you call Pru. Then we're off to the hospital."

Nerves hit me and did it hard.

"I'm scared," I whispered.

"I'm here."

"What if I mess—"

"I'm *here*, sugarpie."

I released a shaky breath.

"It's going to be okay."

"Right." Less whisper and more a quiet word.

But...progress.

"Good?"

I nibbled my lip but nodded. "Good."

Then he was carrying me, ignoring my protests, setting me on the bed and getting me into the outfit I'd set out to wear to the hospital in case something like this happened (I was either very prepared or had ESP). He changed as I phoned Pru.

Another contraction hit mid-call, so he took over, relaying the info, promising to meet them at the hospital.

Because he was Raph.

Because he was *mine*.

"Right," I whispered when it was done. "I think it's go time."

He kissed my forehead. "You got this."

A breath. My hand tight in his. "I know I do." I smiled. "Because you're here."

"Fuck, I love you."

"I love—"

Another contraction hit.

And then it really *was* go time.

EPILOGUE

Raph

SHE'D BEEN MAGNIFICENT.

She was *still* magnificent, hair a mess, lipstick chewed off, head pressed back into the pillows, eyes closed.

Her fingers were still wrapped tightly around mine, even as she took a much-deserved nap.

A breast pump sat on the rolling table, because of course, my woman was going to try to do that for the babies.

Catherine Hazelbeth and Leonardo Oliver Aubert had made their entrance healthy, albeit a bit on the small side. Mom and Dad were currently with them in the NICU for some precautionary testing, but the doctors didn't expect it to take longer than an hour or two.

And Beth, who'd just pushed out two babies, had cried when she heard the names.

Then cried some more when she had watched Pru and Marcel holding them.

But her tears had dried when she held them, softly

brushing her finger over their downy cheeks. "I'm going to be your favorite auntie," she whispered. "We're going to have *all* the fun and give your mommy and daddy all the gray hairs."

Then she looked at me. "Can you take them? My arms—" She'd been tired, so tired she could barely hold them. And I knew that while *she* knew they weren't her babies, they also *were*, would always be in many ways.

I felt the same.

The babies were mine, but not.

So, I held them before their parents had reclaimed them, and then I held her hand, read up on pumping breastmilk, and stayed with Beth while she slept.

A while later, her lids slid open. "I want our own," she whispered, sending my heart pounding as her eyes connected with mine. "We'll rock it as aunt and uncle, but we're going to kill it as parents."

I tucked my phone away then smoothed back her hair, smiled at the woman who owned me. "Plus, it'll be fun putting in the effort to make them."

She grinned, but then started to sit up. "I should—"

"Rest." A squeeze of her hand. "You should rest and recover your strength and then get back to the *I shoulds*."

"Right," she whispered, lids already struggling to stay open. "When did you get so smart?"

"Probably around the time I watched you push those babies out, sugarpie."

Her head tilted toward me, a blip of uncertainty. "Was it too much?"

"It was the most beautiful thing I've ever seen, honey."

"Oh."

"Though Pru and Marcel holding them was a close second."

Beth's face gentled. "They'll be great parents."

"They already are."

"Yeah." Her eyes closed. "Mila is so wonder—" She broke off on a yawn.

I smoothed her hair again, coaxed her to sleep, and then when her eyes were closed, I glanced down at her hand in mine.

And smiled.

And...wondered how long it would take for her to realize that I'd just slipped a giant ass diamond ring on her finger.

Or to see the cooler of beers Pru had left by the door.

"You KNOW," she whispered, a week later, curled up beside me in bed. "I'm really not minding having my body back."

"Because of the ability to drink beer?"

"Well, that," she said, cuddling closer, "and because this fits."

She held up her hand, my diamond glittering in the pale light.

"Does that mean you've finally noticed it?"

In fairness, the moment her eyes had landed on the ring, she'd softened, eyes going damp, and she'd leaned up to kiss me.

Acceptance without words.

Though, a yes wouldn't have been remiss.

Except, then Pru and Marcel had come back, and Beth had begun pumping, and then there had been feedings and diaper changes and checks by nurses and doctors.

The days had been a blur of activity, and by the time she and I had made it home, we'd slept for what felt like two full days—and that was without having to care for two tiny humans. Still, Beth was pumping like a champ, the twins were growing, Mila Rose had adjusted without incident, and Pru and Marcel had gone from a family of two to five in just a few months.

"Maybe," she murmured, grinning as she rotated her hand from side to side. "It *is* very sparkly, and you know how much I like that."

"Pain in my ass," I muttered.

She burrowed into my side. "One you love."

"Damn right I do. You're *my* pain in the ass."

"You're *so* romantic," she teased.

Solemn eyes. "Is that why you haven't said yes?"

Her fingers traced nonsensical patterns on my chest. "Well, I mean, technically, you just shoved a ring on my finger—one, I'm just saying, that was swollen so that it was impossible to get said ring off—and left it at that. You haven't actually asked."

That was true.

So, I rolled us, sliding off the edge of the bed, drawing her to her feet and taking myself down on one knee.

"My fierce protector, my ball-buster, my beautiful, smart, *strong* woman"—I kissed the ring on her finger—"you were a dream, a fantasy, and somehow I was lucky enough for you to become my reality."

Tears—more happy ones—dripped down her cheeks. "Raph," she warned.

"You wanted romance, honey, but I can only give you the truth." I kissed her palm, the inside of her wrist, her pulse rapid fire against my lips. "You're my heart."

She inhaled. "Raph."

"You're my soul and my hopes for the future and my happiness in the now, and so I'm asking you— No. Maybe I'm *begging* you to be my wife."

A sniff, her hand dashing across her cheeks, wiping away the tears, and she nodded.

"Is that a yes?"

Another sniff. "I mean, technically you still didn't ask the question."

I grinned, nipped lightly at the inside of her wrist. "A smart ass even when I give her romance."

Dancing blue eyes. "You like my ass."

"I love it." A beat and then I gave her what she needed—because I always would. "Will you marry me, Beth Mason?"

Her hand on my cheek. "I would love to marry you, Raphael Gomez. You're my forever, my always. You looked at the broken pieces of me and somehow thought they were beautiful, and I promise, *promise* that I will do the same for you. Forever and always."

Now my eyes were wet.

But I didn't give a fuck that the wet escaped, not when she was in my arms, my ring on her finger, her mouth on mine, her body pressed tight.

This was my future.

And I couldn't wait to live every moment of it.

Jules

I hefted the bag of trash out through the backdoor of CeCe's.

It was late.

Last call had been made.

And all I wanted was to get home to Ethan.

Plus, if I made it home before three, I wouldn't have to pay Mary for another hour. My next-door neighbor was awesome, but money was always tight, and with Ethan going to kindergarten in the fall, things were only going to get more expensive.

Kid was getting bigger.

Which meant the kid was eating more, and he was outgrowing his clothes and his shoes, and—

Every hour I wasn't spending on childcare meant more money to save for clothes and food and, heaven help me, college one day.

I dropped the bag to the ground, tied it off, and then rose on tiptoe to push open the top of the dumpster, having to do it a couple of times before it banged back against the brick wall and stayed in place. I eyed it warily.

It had fallen down and crashed onto my head too many times to count.

But when it remained resting against the wall, I bent for the bag, hefting it up and launching it into the dumpster.

The rim of the dumpster was high and I was short, so even with practice, that took me a couple of tries.

I closed the top, turned back for the bar, brushing my hands off.

All I had left to do was close out a couple of tables, bus a few others, and then I was going to clock out and head home.

Smiling, I tugged open the door to the hallway.

And just that quickly my smile faded.

I sighed, my head falling back, gaze hitting the ceiling. "Jesus Christ, not again."

Cas's ex.

Her name was...Chester? Charmaine? Colette? No. *Chelsea.*

It was Chelsea.

And that woman was a Do Not Engage Zone.

Thus, I didn't say anything, just started to brush by her.

Ethan. New clothes. Shoes. A college fund.

All of which would be really difficult to give my son if I got my ass fired.

Talons gripped my arm.

Okay, long *nails*, but they might as well have been claws, digging in tightly with surprising strength considering the lithe, slender blonde seemed to barely be breaking a hundred pounds.

God, Cas could crush her.

I tugged at my arm, but Chelsea held firm.

"Let go of me."

Chelsea's eyes went wide. "You need to—"

"I don't *need* to do anything." My temper flared. "Let go and *back* up."

"You need to—"

"Again, ma'am, I don't *need* to do anything." I tugged at my arm again. "Except for my job, which"—I glanced down at the talons—"you're stopping me from doing. So...you need to *back up.*"

Outrage across a beautiful face. "Did you just *ma'am* me?"

Wow.

Not touching that one.

Instead, I tugged at my arm. Again. And this time succeeded in freeing myself. Although the action hurt like hell and left me with nail marks—several of them bleeding—on my forearm.

Good times.

Sighing, I stuck out my arm when Chelsea reached for me again, nearly clotheslining the other woman to a halt...and seriously, there was a whole lot of crazy in that girl's eyes. "You need to go home," I tried.

"I need Luca—"

"Who's Luca?" I snapped.

"You know who he is. *Cas.* You always flirt with him and then he watches you and I *know* you're in love with him. I know it and I hate it and you need to leave him alone because he is mine." She pushed against my arm. "*Mine.*"

Apparently, Cas was Luca.

That was...a development.

But I couldn't focus on it. I needed to get home and save that hour of babysitting. Stat. And maybe I needed to get away from this woman who saw what I'd been trying to hide. Because I couldn't have it.

Because—

"Jules?" Matt asked from down at the end of the hallway. "You okay?"

And now I could kiss my boss.

"Not really," I called.

A heartbeat later, he was at my shoulder, heat drifting along my spine, soaking in through my clothes.

"What the fuck?"

Not Matt.

Oh. Boy. That *wasn't* Matt.

I whipped around, saw it was Cas's heat soaking into me, saw that Matt was pushing against the wall, as though he'd been shoved there and was now trying to regain his balance.

By Cas.

"What. The. *Fuck?*"

Shit.

"Cas, baby," Chelsea began.

I turned back and saw that Chelsea's gaze had gone...oh, man, it sent a prickle down my spine. It had gone really *really*... bad.

I cleared my throat. "I'll just go—"

Cas's fingers wrapped around my wrist, and he started to pull me toward him.

Gently, but angling his body so that I could stand behind him, so that he was between me and the crazy in front of him.

And *that*...settled somewhere deep inside, sanded off the rough edges, warmed me. But before I made it all the way behind him, he went tense and something scary emanated from him, filling the air, filling the hall.

On instinct, I froze.

Cas lifted my arm, and the scratches, the *blood* dripping along my forearm hit the light, suddenly much more visible, suddenly much more obvious, and that scary increased. It looked worse than it was. Yeah, it hurt. For sure. But the dripping wounds looked...ghoulish.

And Cas's face...

Frightening.

"What the fuck?" he said a third time and finished drawing me behind him.

"Cas, I need to—"

Cas—*Luca*—spun us around, propelling me down the hall, leaving Chelsea still talking behind us, but I barely heard another word because then I was inside the women's restroom and my arm was in the sink, and Cas was turning on the faucet.

Warm water on my skin.

The volume increasing in the hall...then abruptly cutting off.

And all the while, Cas didn't seem to notice.

His fingers were gentle as they smoothed soap over my skin, rinsing it with the warm water. Then washing it again.

Like him shifting me behind him in the hall, his actions settled deep.

Even though they probably shouldn't.

Even though they probably didn't mean anything except for a good guy looking after someone who was hurt because of him.

Not that I was blaming him—

The water shut off.

He blotted my skin with a paper towel.

Gently. *So* gently.

"I'm okay, you know."

His head tipped up, gaze hitting mine.

But he didn't say anything, just kept blotting until my skin was dry. "You need to be bandaged up," he said, shifting my arm from side to side, "but I don't think any of these need stitches."

"I'm fine."

Eyes flickering.

Fingers tightening.

Then slowly, oh so slowly, he lifted my arm, pressed his lips to the inside of my elbow, inhaling deeply enough that I shivered.

"You're cold," he murmured, lips still on my skin.

"No," I whispered.

My voice was husky.

"No?"

Mutely, I shook my head.

"So, if not cold then..." He trailed his lips a little higher, up along the inside of my biceps. I shivered again. "Warm?"

Another shake of my head.

"Hot?"

Yeah, *that* was the one.

And even though I didn't nod, I knew he felt the answer. Because I shivered again and then melted against him.

"Hmm." He dropped the sleeve of my T-shirt that he'd pushed up, pressed his mouth to my throat, tongue flicking out, just the slightest bit.

Not hot.

Molten.

"Jules?" he asked against my skin.

My pulse was thundering beneath my skin, leaving me weak and shaking, my thighs trembling. "Yeah?" I managed.

He lifted his head.

Green, *green* eyes on mine.

Lips parting—mine, his—and he leaned close.

Hot breath on my skin. Spicy male in my nose. His mouth right, right *there*.

Oh God, he was going to kiss me.

Oh God, I wanted him to.

Oh God—

His lips hit mine just as...

The door to the bathroom slammed open.

I hope you enjoyed Raph and Beth's story as I much as I do! The next book in the Breakers Hockey series is BLOWOUT. **I have no time in my life for a man. Least of all a swoony hockey player who is allergic to commitment.**

CLICK HERE TO READ BLOWOUT NOW>

If you want even more big, bearded hockey players who fall hard and fast for the women they love *and* get your Smitty fix, pick up book one in the Grizzlies Hockey series, MARRIED TO NUMBER TWENTY-TWO. **I signed the contract. I just didn't expect her to show up ten years later, ready to cash it in.**

CLICK HERE TO READ MARRIED TO NUMBER TWENTY-TWO NOW>

Read on for a sneak peek below!

Aiden

I wake up to a heavy knock on my condo's front door and glare blearily at my phone in the charger.

"Two in the fucking morning," I mutter, grabbing a pillow and clamping it over my ears. "It's two o'clock in the morning on my fucking birthday, and I have to deal with this shit."

This shit being my neighbors.

It's not the first time they've pounded drunk on my door, desperate for their roommate to let them in to what they think is their apartment.

This was sort of funny the first time.

I remember those days, drinking too much, being dumb.

But after the second and the third—where I gained status into the inner circle and a code to the keypad to their apartment door—it was no longer cute.

Now, six months later and countless times of bailing them out, I'm *so* not in the mood.

Especially when it's my fucking birthday.

The knocking cuts off and I think—*pray*—that they've gotten the hint.

But it's approximately two seconds later when it starts up again.

I glance at my phone again, see that really five minutes have passed, making it two-seventeen and officially my birthday.

Some present.

I could try to ignore it—but that just means extending the torture. Sighing, I toss back the blankets and stomp to my apartment door, whipping it open to reveal a slender brunette on my doorstep.

"Ho, mama," she says, gaze taking a slow perusal down my body.

"Who the fuck are you?"

"It's me. Luna."

I stare at her, uncomprehendingly.

"From Rockfield?" she adds.

Recognition begins to dawn. "Luna Maybelle?"

"Yup! That's me." She nods, grinning, and I see it then, the glimpse of my best friend from the childhood rink I grew up playing at come out in her smile. Mischief and life. Joy and hard work.

Summers spent spending every spare moment together—her figure skating, me playing hockey.

But she's not little Luna anymore.

Christ, she's anything but—tall, beautiful, curves for days—and she's staring at me.

Because I'm staring at her.

Fucking hell.

I spur myself into motion.

"Luna! Oh my God!" I pull her into a hug. "What the hell are you doing here?"

"It's your birthday!" She holds up a piece of paper that looks faintly familiar. "And, well, it's mine too, remember?"

That's right.

We have the same birthday.

"We're both twenty-five, single, and—"

My eyes narrow in on the paper. It's crumpled and stained, as though it's years old.

A purple and pink swirl decorates the edges and suddenly I remember her painstakingly drawing it as we sat side-by-side at one of the high top tables of the ice rink, waiting for the Zamboni to finish cutting the ice.

Her brow had been furrowed. Her movements carefully controlled.

And I had been obsessing over how pink her lips were and

what her butt looked like in her skating dress, so much so that I barely remember what we'd been drawing.

No, I think hard, grabbing on to those memories, not what we'd been *drawing*.

The contract we'd put together.

The contract my hormonal twelve-year-old self had signed.

With a sparkly pink colored pencil.

A giant boulder settles in my stomach, but before I can snap myself out of the horror of those memories, she shoves the paper in my hands then throws her arms around my neck.

"We're getting married!"

CLICK HERE TO READ MARRIED TO NUMBER TWENTY-TWO NOW>

Hate missing Elise's new releases? Love contests, exclusive excerpts and giveaways?
Then signup for Elise's newsletter here!

www.elisefaber.com/newsletter

And join Elise's fan group, the Fabinators (https://www.facebook.com/groups/fabinators) for insider information, sneak peaks at new releases, and fun freebies! Hope to see you there!

If you enjoy my series, considering supporting me on PATREON! Get access to early releases, bonus content, character art, audiobooks, special edition covers, swag, and much more!

CLICK HERE TO SUPPORT ME>

I so appreciate your help in spreading the word about my books, including sharing with friends! Please leave a review on your favorite book site!

ALSO BY ELISE FABER

***Gold Hockey* (all stand alone)**

Blocked

Backhand

Boarding

Benched

Breakaway

Breakout

Checked

Coasting

Centered

Charging

Caged

Crashed

A Gold Christmas

Cycled

Caught

Cap

Covered

Crushed

Changed

Scored

Breakers Hockey (all stand alone)

Broken

Boldly

<u>Breathless</u>

<u>Ballsy</u>

<u>Bewitched</u>

Blowout

Breathe

A Breakers Christmas

Blazed

Bound

Sierra Hockey Series

Over the Line

Caught from Behind

The Big Skate

On the Fly

Rush Hockey Trilogy #1

Big Puck Energy

Filthy Puckboy

So Pucking Over It

Rush Hockey Trilogy #2

Love, Pucks, and Other Stories

All's Fair in Pucks and War

No Pucks Lost Between Us

Rush Hockey Novellas

Puck and Make Up

Eagles Hockey Series (all stand alone)

Broken Laces

Lace 'em Up

Knotted Laces

Loaded Laces

Lucky Laces

Billionaire's Club (all stand alone)

Bad Night Stand

Bad Breakup

Bad Husband

Bad Hookup

Bad Divorce

Bad Fiancé

Bad Boyfriend

Bad Blind Date

Bad Wedding

Bad Engagement

Bad Bridesmaid

Bad Swipe

Bad Girlfriend

Bad Best Friend

Bad Rebound

Bad Romance

Bad Business

Bad Billionaire's Quickies

Love, Action, Camera (all stand alone)

Dotted Line

Action Shot

Close-Up

End Scene

Meet Cute

Love After Midnight **(all stand alone)**

Rum And Notes

Virgin Daiquiri

On The Rocks

Sex On The Seats

Life Sucks Series

Train Wreck

Hot Mess

Dumpster Fire

Clusterf*@k

FUBAR

Perfect Storm

Free Fall

Lost Cause

Roosevelt Ranch Series **(all stand alone, series complete)**

Disaster at Roosevelt Ranch

Heartbreak at Roosevelt Ranch

Collision at Roosevelt Ranch

Regret at Roosevelt Ranch

Desire at Roosevelt Ranch

Phoenix Series (read in order)

Phoenix Rising

Dark Phoenix

Phoenix Freed

Phoenix: LexTal Chronicles (rereleasing soon, stand alone, Phoenix world)

From Ashes

In Flames

To Smoke

KTS Series (all stand alone, series complete)

Riding The Edge

Crossing The Line

Leveling The Field

Scorching The Earth

Cocky Heroes World

Tattooed Troublemaker

ABOUT THE AUTHOR

USA Today bestselling author, Elise Faber, loves chocolate, Star Wars, Harry Potter, and hockey (the order depending on the day and how well her team -- the Sharks! -- are playing). She and her husband also play as much hockey as they can squeeze into their schedules, so much so that their typical date night is spent on the ice. Elise is the mom to two exuberant boys and lives in Northern California. Connect with her in her Facebook group, the Fabinators or find more information about her books at www.elisefaber.com.

facebook.com/elisefaberauthor

amazon.com/author/elisefaber

bookbub.com/profile/elise-faber

instagram.com/elisefaber

tiktok.com/@elisefaberauthor

goodreads.com/elisefaber